Revelation

A Becky White Thriller

Jo Fenton

www.darkstroke.com

Copyright © 2020 by Jo Fenton
Artwork: Adobe Stock © hikolaj2, © Ron Dale
Design: soqoqo
Editor: Sue Barnard
All rights reserved.

.

No part of this book may be used or reproduced in any manner whatsoever without written permission of the author or Crooked Cat Books/darkstroke except for brief quotations used for promotion or in reviews.

First Dark Edition, darkstroke. 2020

Discover us online:
www.darkstroke.com

Find us on instagram:
www.instagram.com/darkstrokebooks

Include **#darkstroke** in a photo of yourself
holding his book on Instagram and
something nice will happen.

To my lovely sons, Michael and Andrew: thank you for letting me bounce ideas around, and for giving me your honest input always. Thank you for being awesome.

Acknowledgements

There are lots of amazing people to thank for making this book possible.

Firstly, as always, I'd like to give credit to my fabulous friend and incredibly talented editor, Sue Barnard. She is a great person to work with, and always makes the editing process flow so easily.

Sue is also one of the Manchester Scribes, who all helped with monthly critiques of the earlier chapters, and made sure I was on the right track. The other awesome Scribes are Pauline Barnett, Louise Jones, Karen Moore, Claire Tansey, Awen Thornber, Helen Sea and Grant Silk.

Another important step in the writing process is Beta Reading. My wonderful beta readers were instrumental in making sure the story worked on all levels, and ensuring there were no plot holes. Huge thanks to Sue Barnard (again), Ray Fenton, Katy Johnson, Susan King, Megan Mayfair, Josh Rose and Gayle Samuels.

Before I started writing Revelation, I didn't know the first thing about martial arts. I would like to extend a hearty thanks to Vikki and George Launders for their help in providing me with some basic training and demonstrating some of the key techniques used in the book. Thanks also to Clare Reynolds for partnering with me in the session. I hope your wrists have fully recovered.

Family are always an essential part of my support network, so I'd like to thank my husband Ray for all his help and advice, reading, sharing ideas, and listening to me waffle, and for doing far more than his share of housework so I could have valuable writing time. Thank you to my boys, Michael and Andrew, to whom this book is dedicated. Their insight into being a male student was hugely helpful.

Thanks also go to my mum, Rhoda Myers, who helped with my final proofread, and provided another valuable pair of ears for me to test my thoughts and ideas.

Last but definitely not least, a massive thank you to my publisher, darkstroke, and particularly to Laurence Patterson and Steph Patterson for believing in me, helping with cover art and marketing advice, and for everything they've done behind the scenes to bring this book out into the world.

About the Author

Jo Fenton grew up in Hertfordshire. She devoured books from an early age and, at eleven, discovered Agatha Christie and Georgette Heyer. She now has an eclectic and much loved book collection cluttering her home office.

Jo combines an exciting career in Clinical Research with an equally exciting but very different career as a writer of psychological thrillers.

When not working, she runs (very slowly), and chats to lots of people. She lives in Manchester with her family and is an active and enthusiastic member of two writing groups and two reading groups.

Revelation

A Becky White Thriller

Glossary

Challah – a traditional Jewish bread, eaten on the Sabbath and other holy days

Hashem – God

Kabbalah – Jewish mysticism – mainly to do with the search for God

Mikvah – baths where a religious Jewish woman would immerse herself once a month before resuming relations with her husband

Shabbat – Sabbath – runs from Friday evening (one hour before Sundown) to Saturday evening at Sundown

Shul – Synagogue

Yarmulke/Kippah – skull cap – head covering for men

Chapter One
Tuesday 24/1/89

Becky

CRIME SCENE - DO NOT CROSS

Yellow tape seals the doorway between the lifts and the east wing of the halls of residence – tenth floor. Instead of diving into the lift to head down for breakfast, I move closer and try to see beyond the tape. But all that's visible is the dimly-lit corridor with doors on either side – the male student bedrooms. One of the doors on the left looks open, but it's hard to tell without breaching the barrier.

Instead I peer into the common room – still accessible, but next to the forbidden area. Four young men are slumped in armchairs, various degrees of distress showing on their faces. Sanjay and Nathan are still wearing pyjamas. Studying Politics and History respectively, they tend not to have early morning lectures and are rarely seen before lunch. Stuart, Dentistry, is dressed for lectures in jeans, black Metallica t-shirt and red and white check shirt. His freckles stand out against the fair skin, several shades paler than usual.

Finally, I allow my gaze to rest on my best friend in Halls. Daniel, tall with dark curly hair, has his knees curled up to his chest, and appears to be staring at his knees. I stumble to his side and put my hand on his shoulder, pulling back slightly as I get close. The stench of his sweatshirt that he wore all last week hits me; he must have grabbed whatever was closest to hand.

He doesn't respond to my touch, so I take a deep breath

and turn to Stuart, who seems the most conscious of the four.

"What's happened? And where's Rick?"

Rick Kennedy is the dish of the house. Six foot two, with blond hair, a smile that would melt diamonds, and the bluest eyes ever; he shares the corridor with the four men present. And he's missing.

"He's dead, Becks." Stuart's voice is hushed.

"What?" I stare at him. A ball of lead settles in my stomach. Rick and I were flirting over pizza and chips in the dining hall only yesterday. My legs threaten to buckle, and I sit down beside Daniel. "He can't be… Are you sure?"

"Dan found him this morning. In his room."

Questions flood through my brain, but my tongue feels suddenly too big for my mouth. I'm unable to form a coherent sentence now, and I hug my knees to my chest, subconsciously mirroring my friend. Stuart doesn't bother asking if I'm okay. No one is.

"Where did you say Rick was found, Stu?" asks Nathan suddenly.

"In his room."

"Rick's room?" Nathan seems alert now, but I don't get his questions. I thought it was obvious.

"Yeah, where else?" says Stuart.

"I reckon Nathan thought Rick might have been in my room." Daniel's voice is muffled against his knees, and sounds as though he has a bad cold.

"You said 'Dan found him… in his room'. Wasn't obvious, mate!" says Nathan. He casts Daniel a covert glance.

I know there have been rumours. Even I don't know if they're true, and I've been friends with Daniel for a few years now – long before we came to Uni. Rationally I don't care if the rumours are true, but the jealousy twisting my gut tells a different story.

Rick was in his own room. Why and how he died is beyond any of us.

The common room is beginning to fill up, as curiosity takes hold of the tenth-floor residents passing the police tape.

"Why are the police here?" asks Michelle from my corridor.

As if in response, a man in a suit appears in the doorway. He has a blond moustache and curly hair that looks like a perm.

"I'm the officer in charge here. How well did you kids know Mr Kennedy?"

Stuart and Nathan seem to bristle at being called kids. The officer doesn't look much more than thirty. I answer before they have a chance to say something rude.

"We've known him about five months, since the start of Uni. He's a nice guy. Friendly with everyone." I don't add that every girl within a five-mile radius fancies him. I don't think PC Permed-Hair-And-Moustache would care. I push the thought away and ask the burning question. "How did he die?"

Everyone in the common room stares at me. Even Daniel raises his head to give me an incredulous look.

"Don't know yet, Miss. Might be drugs. We can't be sure at this stage though. We'll need to take everyone's details. You boys will need to wait until we've searched your rooms before you can go back in. When we're sure none of you have anything to hide, you can go back in there."

I can't get my head round this. Rick is dead. Is there any chance he killed himself? Was it an overdose? It seems so out of character. I didn't know he even took drugs. And this policeman is an idiot. Surely if the boys had anything to hide, they would have put it somewhere 'safe' long before the police were called?

Chapter Two
Tuesday 24/1/89

Daniel

He's dead. How can he be dead?

We were together only yesterday evening, chilling out in my room, listening to music. I know the other guys suspect something's going on. They're wrong. We're just friends.

Shit. We WERE just friends. The pain in my chest is worse than any heart attack. Gripping, intense, and impossible to breathe through.

There's some thick policeman in the room, trying to ask everyone questions. His voice is background noise; easily ignored. Becky is at my side, but I know she's watching me. Grey blurs at the edge of my vision. I try to take a deep breath. Failing, I settle for a shallow one. I force a half-smile, trying to reassure Becks. She rests a hand on my shoulder.

"Alright?" she whispers into my ear.

I shrug. We both know I'm not.

I've known Rick one term and a week. We clicked straight away, but it took a couple of weeks for me to fall in love. A fortnight of popping into each other's rooms; sharing our favourite music (Abba, Erasure, Culture Club), discussing the Belgariad books by David Eddings, and catching the bus up to UMIST together – him to go to his Management Science lectures and me for Biochemistry.

By the time we'd watched *The Princess Bride* together at Film Night at the student union, I was his for life.

Life that's been cut short. Hideously short. He was nineteen, for God's sake.

"Are you okay, young man?" The policeman is crouching

down in front of me, with a worried look on his face. Maybe he's not so stupid.

Becky's hand tightens on my shoulder.

"Of course he's not okay. His best mate is dead, and he can't get into his room to grieve in peace." She stands up. "Dan, do you want to lie down for a bit in my room?"

I nod, and she hands over a key. "Go on. Take your time. I'll hang out here for a bit. Do you want to ring home? Maybe you could go back for a couple of days?" Her voice is hesitant. She knows I've got a ropey relationship with my dad. Otherwise it would have been a good idea. Get away from here. Away from all the reminders.

"I need to stay. Thanks though. And yeah, I'll go and hang out in your room for a bit."

The officer stands up to let me pass, and I go along to room 1009, Becky's room.

I fumble with the key; my hands are still shaking. I hadn't realised how much I was trembling when I was in the common room. It probably confirmed all the suspicions of the other guys. What do I care? I don't care about anything any more.

I finally manage to get inside, and go over to the window, kicking aside Becky's dirty washing that litters the floor. She's an old friend, and I'd do anything for her, but she's such a slob. Sometimes I tidy her room up a bit, but it's not important today. Nothing's important, except that Rick's not here any more. God, I can't cope with this.

I stare out of the window, taking in the grey views of a wintry Manchester. The same views that Rick had from his room. That he'll never see again. I squeeze my eyes shut to stem the tears that threaten.

How the hell can he be dead?

Chapter Three
Tuesday 24/1/89

Becky

With a sense of relief, I watch Daniel leave the common room.

It's short-lived. As soon as he's out of earshot, the gossip begins.

"Do you reckon they were having an affair?"

"Are they gay?"

"What if Rick found he's got AIDS?"

"Shut up, all of you! It's none of our business. So what if they were gay? And we don't know either way anyhow. And not everyone who's gay has AIDS. Grow up, for God's sake!" I glare at Nathan, who'd asked this ridiculous question.

A tiny doubt creeps into my mind, and I shove it away.

The policeman has settled himself into an armchair opposite the TV, and appears to be watching *Oprah* with subtitles. A tautness in his bearing suggests he is less interested in the show than he appears. I suspect he's listening intently to our argument and wants us to forget he's there. Several people seem to have granted his wish.

I leave the sofa, and go over to him.

"What are your colleagues doing? Are we needed? Will you be questioning us?"

He gives me an amused and somewhat supercilious smirk.

"My colleagues are checking out the area where Mr Kennedy died. Once they are certain they've collected any clues as to whether this was accident, suicide or murder, they will let me know how they would like to proceed. One of my constables is already getting all your details from the Hall

Warden, so as far as I'm concerned you can all go off to your lectures. I know where to find you." He looks round at the gathering of students on armchairs and sofas dotted around the room. "Don't leave the city without telling us, kids."

There's a murmured response, not all of it polite. The policeman gets up to leave. I put my hand out to detain him a moment.

"Wait. What's your name?" I ask. "In case one of us has any information for you, how do we contact you?"

He hands me a card in silence.

I read it out: "*DI Tom Bannister. Longsight Police Station.*" There's a phone number below. "Are you the nearest to here, Inspector?"

"It was us or West Didsbury. You got us. You should be pleased. We've a much better response rate than they have. Anyway, trot off now. I'm sure you've got classes to go to."

I gaze at his sneering face for a moment. I think I would have preferred the DI from West Didsbury.

I head back to my room patting my pockets for my key. It's only when I get to the door that I remember I gave my key to Daniel. I hesitate. What if he's crying? He might not want me to see. I listen at the door, but can't hear anything. I knock.

There's a shuffling sound, then a bang.

"Shit!" Dan opens the door and stands there rubbing his elbow. "Oh it's you. Come in." He turns and makes his way to the chair by the desk.

I kick a few jumpers out of the way as I head for the bed. I sit back against the wall and look at my friend. His eyes are red but dry. The rest of his face is white, almost grey.

"What happened?" I know it's ambiguous, but I want him to answer the bigger question if he can.

"Tripped over your bloody clothes. Do you have to leave everything in such a mess?"

Okay. So he went for the lesser option.

"Yeah, sorry. I wasn't expecting visitors."

"It's always like this."

"I suppose." The state of my room is not the issue here, and I'm sure he knows it as well as I do. I take a deep breath then say in a gentle voice, "Dan, what happened last night? When you were in his room? You don't have to tell me if you really don't want to, but I want to help you, and I can't do that if I don't know anything."

He gives me a twisted smile. My stomach lurches. That smile always gets to me. It's full of affection, and common sense tells me that's all I'll ever get from him.

"You're a nosy cow, aren't you, Becks? I love you, but seriously?"

Those three words might be the words I've always wanted to hear from him, but not in that context. Anyway, he says it to all his female friends. He's an affectionate soul. But I'm not happy with the adjective. The size of my nose is a sore point.

"Yes, seriously." I give him an anxious glance. I don't reckon he's thought this through, but he needs to be aware. "If it turns out that Rick…" I see Daniel wince at the name. "Sorry, but if it wasn't an accident…"

"He didn't do drugs. He wasn't into it. And he'd have told me if he was depressed or worried enough to do something like… you know, like an overdose. Someone must have killed him." A strange look crosses Dan's face, but I put it down to grief.

"That's my point. If he was killed, you were the last one known to see him alive."

The door slams behind him. I don't think he's angry with me, only with the situation. At least, I hope it's not with me. But I have to find out whether Rick killed himself, or if he was murdered. If only to save Dan. If he's right about Rick's refusal to do drugs, it rules out the possibility of accident. And I'm sure he's too young for it to be natural causes.

I get out a spiral-bound notebook. It hasn't been used before. It's got a picture of me and Dan at the Jewish Society winter ball taped to the inside front cover.

He looks incredible in black dinner jacket, red bow tie and cummerbund. It really suits him. But then, to be honest, most of the guys looked pretty hot that night. I reckon I scrubbed up okay too. The red dress was probably a bit flouncy for me, with the tight bodice, and skirt flowing out from the waist. It made me look a bit like a Barbie doll. But quite a pretty one. At least it hid the bulge of my stomach that I can never quite get rid of. And because the photo is full length and front-facing, it's hard to tell that my nose is too big.

I was so happy that night. Dan had agreed to come to the ball with me, maybe because Rick couldn't go. As it was a J-Soc event, and Rick's not Jewish, I had Dan all to myself for the evening, except when he got chatting to that Kabballah guy. There were a crowd of us hanging out there, to be fair, but Dan stayed at my side most of the time. It was only at the end of the night, when he delivered me to my room with a peck on the cheek, a hug and a whispered "Happy Chanukah", that I realised he hadn't seen it as a date.

I shake myself. Enough of the reminiscing. There's a job to do. I turn the front cover back on itself so I can only see the first page. Distractions are not helpful.

I start writing…

24/1/89.
Rick was found dead this morning. Police are checking his room for evidence and don't yet know if it was suicide, accident or murder. They suspect drugs. Dan was the last known person to see him. Dan has ruled out drugs.

Bloody hell. Is that all I know? I'm going to have to find out more about Rick. I don't think Dan will tell me. I need to do some proper detecting. Perhaps I can dig out some information from our house tutor, Martin Fielding.

Chapter Four
Tuesday 24/1/19

Daniel

After leaving Becky's room, I go down to the ground floor. The lift's empty, thank God. I don't think I could bear to make small talk right now. I go outside and am greeted by an icy blast. Shit. I came out without a coat. Going back inside is not an option right now. I do not want to see anyone. I shove my hands into my sweatshirt pockets and walk quickly, heading south, away from Halls. There's a tightness in my chest that has nothing to do with the weather.

After a few minutes, I start running. It warms me up and stops me feeling too much. The tightness eases a bit as I focus on running, and trying not to get run over at the zillions of busy junctions between Fallowfield and Withington. By the time I get as far as the cinema, I'm quite warm, but snowflakes are dancing lazily to the ground around me. I've got a choice of roads to go down, or I can go back to Halls, and back to a reality I can't handle.

I turn and look back up Wilmslow Road. On my right is Chicago Diner – home of the best hot chocolate fudge cake in Manchester. I gaze in at the window. Rick and I were here two days ago. Like, Sunday, seriously! Sodding hell.

A black cloud closes in over me.

I open my eyes. I'm on snowy ground and a crowd of people are peering down at me. A sore spot on my head draws my hand to it. My fingers come away sticky and red. Blood. The crowd swims, and when I open my eyes again they're gone. All except one guy. A dark-haired, dark-eyed bloke of maybe about thirty. He looks vaguely familiar.

"Are you alright?" he says.

Clearly I'm not. I'm bleeding to death, and in pieces over the death of the man I love, but then, why would this guy know that? Okay, he can probably see I'm bleeding. He doesn't know I faint at the sight of... He goes a bit blurry.

"Come on, it's not that bad. Stay with me. It's only a scratch. You must have knocked yourself out on the lamp-post. Scalp wounds tend to bleed a bit. Here. This hankie's clean. I'll hold it on for you."

His hands are strangely gentle, but the wound is sore. It's snowing heavily now, and I realise the almost-stranger has covered me with his coat. It's a thick black leather. Good quality. He's in a pin-stripe suit, shirt and tie. He must be frozen. I still can't place him.

"I think I'm okay to get up. Maybe I should get inside. I can get a bus back to Halls." Back to that bloody common room, and that awful policeman, and reality. I force myself into a sitting position. The guy is still holding his hankie to my head. He moves it away and inspects it, keeping it out of my field of vision. I see his arm moving, but he turns so I can't see any red. Even thinking about it makes me feel a bit wobbly, but I concentrate on staying upright as the snow swirls around me, dizzying without any help from head injuries and red stuff. A wave of nausea hits me and I vomit on the ground next to me, managing to avoid the leather jacket – just.

"Hey, it's okay. No bus for you though. I think I should take you to A&E to get that checked out. You might need... attention."

I reckon he was going to say 'stitches' but thought better of it. Nice bloke really. Obviously trying not to make me feel worse. Frankly it would be hard to feel worse. Right now, life is so shit that if fainting would help, I'd be back down on the ground. But it's bloody cold. I'm now shivering, possibly from shock as much as the weather, and I can't get away from the constant stabbing pain in my chest. Rick is dead.

With a bit of help from the guy who I'm sure I've seen somewhere before, I find myself in a posh car. He gets in the driver's seat and turns on the engine.

"I'm Alan, by the way. Alan Rabinowitz. You're Dan, aren't you? We met at the J-Soc ball in December." He grins at me, and memory returns. He was the guy I chatted to for about half an hour. He runs a Kabbalistic group with regular workshops. I vaguely remember promising to attend a couple this term. As this recollection hits me, I feel a strange sense of warmth creeping up my back. Nothing to do with the memory or the grin. The loss of Rick is far too raw for either attraction or embarrassment to penetrate through. I pull myself together to answer.

"I remember. It's hard to recognise people out of context sometimes, and I've hit my head."

The heat is under my bottom now. Have I wet myself? How embarrassing. We're on the way into town. I reckon he's taking me to the Infirmary, but how will I get out of the car? Oh God, I must have wet myself. The whole bloody seat is hot.

Alan glances over at me, and laughs. I must be scarlet. I'm bloody mortified. How can he know?

"Heated seats. Sorry, Dan. I should have warned you. Feels like you've had an accident at first. You get used to it after a bit."

I tentatively touch the leather seat. Warm and dry. I force a smile.

"Yeah, thanks. I've never been in a car with heated seats before."

"There are some tissues in the glove box. Grab them and hold them to your head, can you? I don't want blood on the leather if we can avoid it. And don't worry about the recognition. It happens to me all the time – I must have one of those faces."

"Sorry." I grab a handful of tissues and hold them to the sore point on my head. It's still wet and sticky, and I have to try not to think about what it looks like. If Alan doesn't want blood on his seats, he sure as hell won't want sick on them.

I concentrate on watching the traffic, which has ground to a standstill – unable to cope with half an inch of snow on the road. It takes us nearly an hour to get to the hospital, and my arm is long tired from holding tissues on my head. I've developed a dull headache, and a strong desire for sleep – and oblivion.

Alan doesn't force conversation. Perhaps he realises I'm too exhausted. I hope he's not offended though.

He stays with me in A&E, through the long wait, the local anaesthetic, the stitches, the repeat fainting fit, and finally the discharge back to Halls.

"Come on, Dan. I'll take you back. You're in that tower, aren't you? I think I remember you saying last time we met." He guides me back to the car.

"Yeah. I don't know what I'm going back to." I hesitate. He's basically a kind stranger, despite the events of the last three hours and a half-hour chat at a ball. But maybe I should tell him something, in case he thinks I'm being weird. "One of my friends was found dead this morning. The police are hovering around. They don't know if he... Anyway, they've sealed off all the guys' rooms. We weren't allowed in this morning when I left."

Alan navigates his way out of the car park into a small gap in the heavy traffic.

"You could stay at mine if you want? I live in North Manchester; I'm just down here on business. Just as well, as it turned out."

"No, I'd better get back." It's dawned on me that Becky will be frantic by now. If I don't get to her soon, she's likely to do something stupid, like getting that blasted policeman to track me down. "My friends'll be getting worried. Thanks anyway."

There's a few minutes silence. The traffic is a bit easier in this direction, and it stopped snowing while we were in the hospital. We drive past a funny-looking building known locally as the Toast Rack – a landmark a couple of minutes' drive from my hall.

"Have you got a phone number that I can call you on?" he says. "I'd like to check you're okay. There's a pen and paper in the glove box. I meant to get your number at the ball, after you said you'd like to come to the workshops, but we got interrupted."

I find the required writing materials lurking under the tissues, and scribble my room number and the house phone number on the small sheet of paper.

"It's not always easy to get through. There's one phone between forty-six students, and every evening there's a queue of people wanting to call home. It's hell."

"What about during the day? I take it you won't be going to lectures tomorrow, until your head's better?"

"I won't be hanging around Halls if I can help it. You'd better give me your number, and I'll call you."

He reels off a string of numbers and I scribble them on another sheet of paper, tear it off, and shove it in my jeans pocket. I must try to call him and say thanks. Maybe after I've had a sleep.

First I've got to face Becky.

Chapter Five
Tuesday 14/1/89

Becky

Dan's disappeared. Where the hell is he? The guys have been let back into their rooms, but I've knocked on about five times in the last couple of hours and he's not there. And it's snowing.

PC Plod, alias DI Bannister, has returned to his den in Longsight. At least, I assume that's where he's gone. Rick's room is still sealed off with police tape, but there's no more activity on the corridor. I think the forensic team have gone, but maybe they're coming back later.

A steady churning in my gut sends me out of my room to knock on Dan's door once more. It's gone three now, and I've not seen him since he stormed out of my room earlier. He was in no fit state to roam around by himself. The foyer by the lifts is chilly, and I dig my hands into my sweatshirt pockets for warmth. I'm just opening the door to the boys' corridor, when the lift on the right opens. I pause in hope, but it's Sanjay.

"You okay, Becks?"

"Yeah, just looking for Dan. You've not seen him have you?"

"No. I've been at Uni – I had a tutorial this afternoon. I figured I ought to go."

"Sure. Well, if you see him, can you knock on and let me know? I don't want him to think I'm making a fuss, but…"

"Fine. No problem. I'll keep an ear out. He's next door to me, so I'll probably hear him come back."

The left-hand lift door opens, and a shivering, pale Daniel steps out. Sanjay gives a brief wave, and makes a strategic dash towards his room.

My mouth dries up. I want to check he's okay, but he looks exhausted. We stand still and face each other for a long moment. I run a hand through my hair, for the hundredth time today.

"Sorry. I didn't mean to worry you," he says with a half-hearted smile. "Been a hell of a day. Got any hot chocolate?"

"Yeah, sure. Do you want to go to your room? It's tidier than mine, and you can lie down on your own bed. I'll bring the drinks in a minute and knock on."

"Thanks."

Five minutes later, armed with two mugs of steaming Cadbury's hot chocolate, made with milk as a treat, I give Dan's door a kick.

"Hey, it's me. I've not got any hands free."

He opens the door. He's wearing pyjamas.

"Sorry, Becks. I didn't think you'd mind. I feel like shit, and want to get into bed properly. Happy for you to stay though while we have the chocolate." He takes one of the mugs, and puts it on his spotless bedside table. I sit in the chair next to the desk, and remove a packet of chocolate hobnobs from my sweatshirt pocket.

"Fancy a biscuit? I was keeping them for a rainy day. Or a snowy day as it turned out." I pass him the pack.

"Feel a bit queasy, but one'd be good. Cheers."

I look steadily at him as he nibbles at the biscuit. He's missing quite a lot of hair at the back. He's got a curly mop on top, and been shorn at the back and sides. It looks weird, particularly with the white medical dressing covering the shorn part.

"What happened? You're obviously injured. I'm assuming you've been to hospital?"

"Yeah. I fell over, banged my head and knocked myself out. I'm a bit squeamish, so I didn't feel great when I came round. A guy took me to the hospital and waited with me."

"A stranger? Why would he do that? I mean, I would if it was a girl that got injured, but I didn't think guys did that sort of thing."

"Well, he did. I guess he's just nice, and actually he wasn't a total stranger. Do you remember that bloke I chatted to at the ball? The Kabbalistic guy? It was him. He was really kind to me. I needed that today." He looks me at awkwardly. "Sorry, I don't mean you. You're always nice to me. I can't explain how I feel about… what happened to… to Rick. It's beyond shit." His eyes glisten, and I glance away. "I can't even talk about it. But I feel physically ill. And I felt ill before I collapsed and hit my head."

Collapsed? I thought he'd slipped and fallen in the snow. I watch him as he has a sip of chocolate. He's struggling to swallow; I can see his Adam's Apple bobbing up and down as he tries to get the drink down his throat.

"I'm going to let you get some sleep. Do you want any paracetamol or anything?"

"I've got loads. They gave me them at the hospital. Thanks. I'll try to sleep. I just need to not think."

I take my mug and I'm about to grab the biscuits. "Do you want me to leave these? In case you get peckish later?"

"You sure?"

"Yeah. You need them more than I do." I reach over and touch him on the shoulder. "Come find me if you need me. Or if you're ill, knock on the wall. Sanj'll come and get me."

He nods, and I leave him to sleep, closing the door quietly behind me.

It's four o'clock. I had no lunch between my grief for Rick and worry about Daniel. It appears that worry was the overriding emotion, because now that Dan's back in his room, my stomach is rumbling loud enough to be heard 200 miles away in London. The dining room won't open for at least another forty-five minutes, and I need to take my mind off the hunger pangs.

I could sit in my room and think about why Rick might have killed himself, but the thought of it makes me feel sick (as well as hungry – it's a strange combination, but it's exactly how I feel).

I perch on my favourite chair in the common room. It's by

the window, overlooking a quad, and some more Halls. In the distance, when the weather's good, I can see the Cheshire hills, but they're not visible today. It's snowing again.

A couple of guys from Floor Eleven are playing cards on the other side of the room. I don't know them well – they're not part of my group of friends, and there's a strange divide between the tenth and eleventh floors, even though we're technically part of the same house. I watch them for a few minutes. They seem oblivious to what's happened – the fact that on the floor below them, maybe even the bedroom below them, a young man was found dead. How can they not know? Or maybe they do know, but don't care. That's even worse.

One of them looks up. I think his name's Greg, but I'm not sure.

"What's up? Why are you staring at us like that?"

"Do you actually know what happened today?"

Greg raises an eyebrow. "No. Should we?"

"Yes, you bloody well should know!" I swallow hard and sit up straight. Anger and grief close my throat for a moment. Taking a deep breath to stop my voice shaking, I explain. "Rick's dead. He was found this morning." I debate whether to mention drugs, but decide it wouldn't be fair to Rick.

"Seriously?" says the other guy, a blond, athletic lad whose name I really can't remember.

"Of course 'seriously'! I wouldn't make something like that up. It's not a joke. Rick is dead." I don't bother to keep the disgust from my voice.

"We were at a nine o'clock lecture this morning. We only got back half an hour ago." Greg indicates himself and his friend and puts the cards down. "Sorry, Becky. Sean didn't mean to offend you. It's a bit of shock to hear something like that. He was a friend of yours, wasn't he?"

Tension leaves my shoulders and I relax back in the chair. At least Greg isn't a complete jerk. I'll reserve judgement on his pal.

"Yeah, he was one of the crowd. We chatted quite a bit." Flirted too, but they don't need to know that. I didn't really fancy him. We just had a laugh. He couldn't compete with

Dan in my affections.

Greg and Sean look at each other, probably both hoping the other will come up with something appropriate to say. They're spared by the entrance of Martin, our house tutor. Short with grey-brown wispy hair and glasses, he has a faint look of Robin Williams, but lacks the sense of humour.

"Becky, do you have a moment?" he says.

"Yeah sure."

He glances at his watch. "It's nearly four-thirty. We can go and sit in the canteen."

Sounds like a good plan to me. I follow him to the lift, and half-listen as he makes boring and irrelevant small talk about the weather. Tension is palpable, as it's obvious that's not why he wanted to talk to me.

When we get to the canteen, it's empty except for the catering staff, and they're not serving food yet. We grab seats at the edge of the dining area, not too far from where the food will be served. Seated opposite him, I wait for him to start. I've plenty of questions of my own, but with Martin, it's better to let him get warmed up.

"Sorry to pull you out of the common room, Becky, but I felt it would be better to speak quietly."

"Yes of course." I look at him expectantly. He's rubbing his hands together as if cold. Actually it is freezing in here, but there's sweat forming on his upper lip.

"How well did you know Rick?"

"A crowd of us went drinking and clubbing a lot. A couple of times a week anyway. We were part of the same group. Friendly, but not close buddies." There's so much more I could say, but I'll wait for him to ask.

He rubs a hand on the back of his neck. He's looking really uncomfortable.

"I hope you don't mind me asking, but a lot of the girls are less approachable than you. You're very easy to talk to." Crikey. I wouldn't think it, the way he's acting now. He can't even look at me. His eyes are fixed on the table between us. "I understood from things that were said before… I mean before today… that a lot of girls found Rick very attractive."

I take pity on Martin. "Yeah. Loads of girls fancied him. I wasn't one of them. He wasn't my type. We got on okay and had a laugh. He was a good guy. Although I wasn't close to him, he was the type you could trust to get you safely back to your room if you were drunk, and he wouldn't take advantage. So yes, I liked and respected him. I think everyone did."

"Was he into drugs? He didn't appear to be, but appearances can be deceptive."

"I've never seen any signs of it. He didn't seem the type." I'm not sure what the type is, but if Dan says Rick didn't do drugs, that's good enough for me.

"Do you think he might have been depressed? The police were asking, and I had to admit I didn't know."

"There were no outward signs of it." I hesitate. The person who would know best is holed up in his room trying to sleep after the day from hell. I won't throw Daniel to the lions though. Even the relatively harmless lion that is sitting in front of me now.

I change tack. "Shall we get some food?"

A few students are piling burgers and chips on to their plates. It's time to join them. I choose lasagne and salad, as it's easy to eat and hard to ruin. My veggie friends struggle regularly with their choices, and I spare a sad glance at the sloppy mess that is parading as the veggie option – it looks like some sort of moussaka, but who knows? Rick was veggie. Maybe they should have put on a decent meal in his honour today. I can't believe he was driven to suicide by the bad food though. We have plenty of external choices, and the options of pizza and veggie burgers at the nearby takeaways prevent starvation.

Seated with the food, I concentrate on eating until the worst of the hunger pangs are settled. I'm a little shaky, given this is the first time I've eaten since dinner last night. I don't think a couple of chocolate hobnobs count.

The time spent in collecting dinner has given me time to think. I have my own questions.

Chapter Six
Tuesday 24/1/89

Daniel

A thumping wakes me up. Is it my head? That feels as if someone's attacking me with an axe, but there's noise associated with this thumping.

"Dan, there's a call for you, mate. And there's a queue a mile long for the phone, so don't take all day. Christ knows how they got through."

I drag myself out of bed, ignoring the dizziness and praying I won't fall down or throw up. Both options are very possible. By the time I've grabbed my key and dressing gown, left the safety of my room, and stumbled to the lift foyer where the phone is located, I'm sweating and can barely stand. I flop onto the step and grab the phone receiver.

"Hello?"

"Dan? Is that you? It's Alan here. From this afternoon?"

"Oh, hi. How did you get through? There are about six people out here waiting to use the phone." A polite warning to be quick seems appropriate, together with a hint that our conversation isn't private.

"Must have struck lucky. How are you doing, anyway?"

"I was having a sleep, but I guess I needed to wake up. What time is it?"

"Just gone six. Are you going into Uni tomorrow?"

"I don't know yet. Depends." I'm not going to spell it out. There are several people still hanging around the lift area, and I have no doubt they're listening hard.

"If you're not going in, can I come and see you?"

This doesn't seem like a come-on. Alan's not gay as far as I can tell, and I'm generally a good judge. Keen to get him off the phone, I arrange for him to come round tomorrow afternoon. Wednesday afternoons are free to allow students to play sport, so I won't have any lectures or labs whether I feel okay or not. As soon as I hang up, Nathan and Stuart, who are lurking nearby, crowd in on me.

"Friend of yours, Dan?" says Nathan.

I hate the smirk on his face, but don't have the energy to fight. Instead, I shrug and push past them. If I don't get back to bed soon, I might throw up. Whilst it would teach the bastards a lesson, it wouldn't help my cause. Without replying to their jeers, I return to my room and collapse on the bed.

What does Alan want with me? He sounded like he was really keen to see me, but I don't think I made that good an impression. He's not even a student. I suppose I should be suspicious, but he just seems like a nice guy who was giving a helping hand.

I'm desperately fighting the thoughts that are battering at the edges of my exhausted brain. My chest is hurting already, and I know that as soon as I let the thoughts in, the pain will become unbearable. I can't deal with it tonight. My vision blurs with bitter, salty tears. I turn on to my side and curl up, hugging my knees in a vain attempt to keep out the agony. It's not working.

Shit. Rick, why did you leave me? You knew I loved you. I never said it, but I didn't think I had to. Why the fuck would you kill yourself?

Grief overwhelms me, and I howl like a baby who's lost its mum.

Minutes or hours pass. I've no idea how many. My pillow is soaked, my throat's sore, and my head hurts even more than it did when I woke up, though with a more generalised ache. The tightness in my chest hasn't eased. Crying doesn't relieve grief. It just adds a whole load of physical symptoms to compete with the emotional ones.

A sudden urge to move drives me to the window. The

courtyard below is lit. I want to escape, but the window has a stupid safety bar that prevents it opening more than a crack. Could I jump from the tenth floor? I don't think I'd have the courage.

In a bid for distraction, I pick up a novel: Piers Anthony – *Incarnations of Immortality – Fate*. Bloody hell. Twenty-four hours ago, Rick and I were comparing notes on this very book. He finished it last week – I'm halfway through. I try to read, but my vision is too blurred.

It's going to be a long night.

Wednesday 25/1/89

My alarm goes off at eight am as usual. I don't reckon I slept for more than a few short stretches. My eyes feel like sandpaper from all the crying, and the bump on the back of my head hurts like hell. I can't face lectures this morning. Apart from exhaustion and the extreme risk of bursting into tears in the middle of lectures, I would either have to remove the dressings from my head (my stomach contracts at the thought), or face the questions and curiosity from my course-mates. I make a mental note to ask Becky to help with the dressings later, and turn over to try to catch up on some sleep.

I wake up some time later feeling a bit less crap. The alarm clock on my bedside shows just after midday. A plan for getting through the rest of the day is needed, but I have no idea what to do. All I know is that Alan is due to visit at about two, and I look like shit. A brave glance in the mirror over the sink at the end of the bed confirms my suspicions. Black rings under my eyes, a two-day growth of stubble, and a bloody awful haircut from when they had to shave for the stitches. I'd get arrested for something if I showed my face like this. If Alan is kind enough to check up on me, the least I can do is wash and shave.

I manage to get to the bathroom without being seen. I reckon the others aren't back from morning lectures yet. None of them are particularly into sport, so I need to be quick, but I have a quick dip in the bath, keeping the back of my head dry. I vaguely remember them telling me to keep the dressings on and dry for a week. God only knows how I'm going to wash my hair in that time, but as Rick's no longer around to see me, I don't suppose I care. Maybe it's better that Alan visits today, before my hair becomes too gross. I'll just have to turn into a hermit for the next week.

Washed, shaved and dressed, I look and feel a bit better by the time there's a knock on my bedroom door. It's only just gone twelve-thirty though. I open the door to see Becky standing there with two big pizza boxes and two cans of coke.

"Lunch. Can I come in?" She suits actions to words and brushes past me, plonking the food and drink on the desk. "Okay if I sit down?"

I nod, and then regret it, as it sets my head to violently aching again. I straighten up the navy duvet over the bed. Headache or not, I can't invite people into a messy room, not even Becks, who's the messiest person I know.

Once we're both sitting down, her on the chair and me on the bed, she passes me a box and a can. My stomach gurgles a bit. Not quite a rumble – my emotions are too ropey for me to be properly hungry.

"Eat," she says, pointing at the box. "You've barely eaten for two days. I got you tuna and mushroom, your usual, right?"

"Thanks Becky. It's really good of you. I'll pay you back as soon as I've been to the cashpoint."

"Forget it. Least I can do. Now eat, or you'll be passing out when your new friend comes to visit."

"How do you know?" I rack my mushy brains trying to remember if I've seen her since I made the arrangement with Alan, but I'm pretty sure I've not.

She wrinkles her nose. "Bloody Nathan. Sat next to me at breakfast and started quizzing me about who was coming to see you this afternoon. I told him it was none of his business and ignored him for the rest of the meal. I had to rush anyway; I was a bit late down this morning."

"How did you figure out it was a new friend?" Curiosity wins out over annoyance. I hate everyone knowing my personal business.

"Elementary, my dear Watson," she says with a flourish. "You were rescued by a kind man yesterday, albeit not quite a stranger. He wanted to check up on you. Nathan said it was a man's voice on the phone, and that he asked for you as Dan. According to you, your dad always calls you Daniel. Therefore it had to be a friend. If he was persistent enough to break through the mayhem of phone calls last night, then it had to be someone who's really concerned about you. Now eat!"

I obey, somewhat in awe of her deductive skills, and we munch in silence for a while. I only manage two slices, and have to force the second one down, but I do feel less light-headed afterwards.

"I don't know much about Alan. Do you think it's stupid to let him come into my room? I don't want to take him into the common room though."

Becky looks thoughtful for a moment. "I don't suppose you want me to stick around?"

"Sorry." I smile at her to take any sting away. It's not a rejection. "As I said, I barely know him. Introducing him to any friends might be seen as a bit weird. He's just coming to check up on me."

She goes to the window. "Snow's melted. Why don't you take him to the pub? Are you still wobbly, or are you up to walking that far?"

"That's not a bad idea. It's only ten minutes' walk. Thanks."

As if on cue, there's a knock on the door. I check my watch. If it's him, he's twenty minutes early. I take a deep breath and open the door. Alan's standing in the corridor, wearing black jeans, a shirt, scarf and a leather jacket. Becky escapes from the room with her pizza box and a murmured apology.

"Hi Alan. I'll just grab my coat. We can go to the pub if that's okay?"

Chapter Seven
Wednesday 25/1/89

Becky

Back in my own room with half a pizza and a lot to think about, I take out my notebook and sit on the bed.

Martin's information about Rick was pretty limited. I jot it down anyway.

Richard Kennedy. Born 18 November 1969. Grew up in Abingdon, near Oxford. Attended private school. Family moved to Edinburgh in the last couple of years. Applied to study Management Science with predicted grades of 3 As in History, Economics and English.

That's great, but it doesn't tell me a thing about Rick of any importance. Does it? Well maybe a little bit. He obviously comes from a wealthy family. Oxford is an expensive place to live, and although he might have had a scholarship for school, there was a faint arrogance about him that suggested he didn't know or understand poverty. I'm a bit curious as to why his family moved to Edinburgh, but it's probably not relevant.

I'm thinking of him now in the past tense. How horrible. My brain seems to have got used to the idea that he's not with us any more, but my gut and heart haven't caught up yet. I can't begin to understand how Dan felt – they were virtually inseparable.

What else do I know? Not a lot.

A tap on the door interrupts my brain-searching. I get up to see who it is, and am surprised to find Martin in the corridor.

He's sweating, and looks even more anxious than he did at dinner yesterday.

"Is everything okay?" I ask. Stupid question really. It obviously isn't.

"The police have released the contents of the room to Rick's family. They're coming tomorrow morning, but I have meetings for the rest of the day. I can't ask anyone else, but you're a trustworthy young woman. Would you mind?"

"I'm happy to help, but I'm not sure what you're asking me to do?"

"I'm afraid the room needs to be emptied." A flush creeps up Martin's face. "The hall authorities have a waiting list, and they want to prepare the room." He coughs. "Would you, er, could you get all his things packed up ready to hand over to his mum and dad tomorrow? I believe there are suitcases in his room. Just pack it all in the cases. If you need any bags…"

I realise he's been holding something in his hand, trying to keep it hidden behind his back. Now he reveals the contents: a roll of black bin-liners. I understand his embarrassment. The tight bastards who run the Halls want the money for the room, even though they've probably been paid for this term already. They've forced poor old Martin to put everything of Rick's into these bags. It's disgusting, but it's not Martin's fault.

Actually, this gives me an opportunity I couldn't have foreseen…

Ten minutes later, I'm inside Rick's room. I shut the door behind me. I do not want to be observed or disturbed doing this. The police must have left it as it was (except for the body), because it still has a very lived-in look. Like all the rooms I've seen in the Tower, the paintwork is a bit tired, and the carpets are grubby and old. The curtains are worn in places.

There's still some dark grey powder around the room, presumably from fingerprint testing. The windowsill is clear, but up here on the tenth floor the windows barely open enough to let in a breeze, so there's no way an intruder could have got in that way. He or she could only have got in through the door. On the desk the powder has gaps. I try to imagine what might have been taken by the police. There are three blank areas: a large round object, perhaps a bottle. Alcohol? Fruit squash? Bleach? I'd hazard a guess at the alcohol. Maybe whiskey. The second blank is a much smaller area, rectangular with slightly rounded edges. A pill bottle? Is my brain focussing on this type of thing because of the suspicion of drugs? I can't even remember who suggested that now.

The third gap is a longer rectangle, maybe 2-3 inches long by half an inch wide. The powder looks as if it's been moved a bit, so the edges are fuzzy. I'm going cross-eyed trying to imagine what might have lain there, so I turn my attention to the rest of the room.

Pyjamas are strewn across the bed. I raise my eyebrows. They're the flannel type, much the same sort of thing my dad wears in winter. I would have expected Rick to wear something a bit more youthful.

I take my camera from my sweatshirt pocket. It's a slim Kodak that fits without being too conspicuous; a present from my brother, Ian, for my eighteenth birthday. Ian finished University last year and is working in a law firm doing his training. "For when you're out investigating, Becks," he said when I opened the parcel. It was a reference to years of playing 'police detective'. It seems strange to be doing it for real now. I've got a spare film canister too, but I leave it in my pocket for now.

I take photos of every aspect of the room, from the powder on the desk, to the door handle, to the mud on the carpet, and the tin foil with the chocolate cake crumbs, with a note saying, '*Enjoy the late night treat, Rick. You've earned it. Thanks for all your help the other night, love and kisses*'.

There's a squiggle at the bottom of the note, which could be anything. I fold the tin foil as neatly as I can, and add it to my pocket, together with the note.

I'm shocked that forensics haven't taken this away for investigation, but perhaps they took what was left of the cake and left the crumbs and the foil. I would like to assume they've also assessed the mud, but who am I to tell them their job?

With all the photos taken, I return the camera to my pocket, and take a deep breath. I need to start packing his stuff away. Under the bed (already photographed) is a huge black suitcase. I place it on top of the bed, and open it up. It's empty except for a bunch of letters behind the mesh in the lid. I wouldn't have spotted them if they hadn't moved when I opened the case. They're held together with an elastic band. It's too much for my curiosity, and I remove the band and look inside the top envelope.

My eyes open wider. The letter, from someone called Joanna in Scotland, contains explicit details of a love life I wouldn't have begun to imagine. Acts that I've just about heard of, but never experienced, are described in vivid imagery. The lady has a way with words. I thought it took a lot to make me blush, but I appear to have been mistaken!

I put the letter back inside the envelope, and examine the outside. On the back there is a return address. An important decision is required. Do I return these letters to the sender, or leave them in the suitcase for Rick's parents to find? If I was Rick, I wouldn't want anyone to see these. The banded pack finds its way into the large expanse of pocket in the front of my sweatshirt, cushioning my camera.

Returning to my allocated task, I start emptying drawers. Clothes are neatly folded, so it's little effort to transfer them to the suitcase. Indicators of his personality and choices fascinate me. His hidden clothing tends to be traditional – Y-fronts instead of boxers, black socks, spotless and ironed white handkerchiefs. On the outside, he always wore stylish and trendy items – slogan t-shirts for Uni, brightly-coloured and ostentatious shirts for going out, designer jeans, smart boots rather than shoes.

This raises an interesting question, of course. Does the clothing reflect a dual personality? Not in the medical sense, although technically that could be possible, but more in the nature of the guy? Was the extrovert persona that we knew a cover for an introverted and conventional young man? The letters from Joanna would suggest she knew the extrovert. Which Rick did Dan know? Dare I ask him? Maybe not yet.

With all the clothes neatly folded in the suitcase (or as neatly as I can manage), I turn to the other items: books, cassettes, Walkman, chessboard, toiletries. There are no obvious clues here. The books are mostly sci-fi/fantasy/gothic horror – also a favourite genre of Dan's. Music tends towards the more depressing variety, in my opinion: original cassettes from The Smiths, Alison Moyet and Depeche Mode, and a number of compilations, listing song choices that would seem to appeal more to the Y-fronts and folded hankies than to the flamboyant shirts.

As I pile things into a second suitcase, I begin to wonder if suicide is a realistic verdict. But then, lots of people listen to sad and melancholic songs and are drawn to gothic novels without killing themselves.

I've always been led to believe that studying a murder victim is the key to solving most murders, or identifying whether murder is the correct verdict, so I'll continue to pursue this line of enquiry. My camera has been active throughout the packing process. I now have photos of all the books, tapes and personal items – even down to the packet of condoms hidden in his drawer. These provided another dilemma. Would his parents want to see these? Reluctant to give them any more pain than necessary, the packet joins my camera and the letters from Joanna in my large pocket. I hope nothing else of dubious parental interest turns up though. I'd struggle to hide anything further.

What else have I discovered in Rick's room? I take a last look round. Everything is packed away in one of the two cases, or in a black bin liner (for bed linen, towels, and the laundry bag that was lurking in the corner behind the sink). Rick was a tidy young man, generally deemed thoughtful to his friends and acquaintances. I glance at the desk where I found the cake. Would he have taken this way out and not left a note? I don't believe so. The character clues I've discovered here suggest only a complex sort of guy with many facets to his personality. There was no evidence of medication, legal or otherwise, except for the gaps showing that the police had taken items away after spreading their powder around.

An uneasy feeling settles in my gut. I take out the camera once more. There are three shots left.

I take close-ups of the powder, one for each missing item. Then I put my fingers on the powder and raise it to my nose. There's no smell to it. I tentatively put a tiny amount on my tongue – it has no taste either. It feels slightly metallic.

Chapter Eight
Wednesday 25/1/89

Daniel

The Queen of Hearts is busy, filled with all the students who are neither interested in sports nor inclined to spend a Wednesday afternoon catching up on assignments.

"Grab a seat, mate. What can I get you?" Alan heads straight for the bar, his hand retrieving a leather wallet from his jeans pocket.

I dither for a moment, wanting to impress with my drinking choices, but deciding there's no point getting something I hate, like beer.

"Cider please. Whatever's on tap. Thanks." I survey the room, looking mainly for somewhere to sit, but also checking for faces I know. I'm not sure why, but it doesn't seem appropriate to introduce Alan to my friends at this stage. Becks doesn't count, but even that was barely an introduction.

Spotting an empty table in a corner, I point it out to Alan, before making a quick dive to save the seats. There are a few vaguely familiar faces – people that I dimly recognise from J-Soc Friday night dinners, and from the student bop – but no one I know well enough to say hello to. I sit with my back to the window, facing the room, but only so I can see Alan to wave to as he comes over with the drinks.

"How's your head?" he asks, setting the drinks on the table.

"Keeping warm. I reckoned it would avoid a lot of irritating explanations if I kept my hood up. A lot of people think I'm a bit weird anyway."

"Why's that?" Alan sits opposite me and gives me a curious glance. He seems genuinely interested, and feeling the loss of Rick, my usual confidant, I open up more than I normally would.

"I don't generally chat a lot. I'm not into football or rugby, not even to watch on TV, and most of my friends are girls – except for Rick. He's the one…" I tail off with a sudden lump in my throat. The tightness has returned to my chest.

"It's alright, mate. I remember you said yesterday that he'd passed away suddenly. I wish you long life."

"Thanks." It feels uncomfortable being the recipient of that. It's what we say to the family if a relative dies. I'm not related to Rick. I don't think being in love with someone qualifies. Especially if it's a secret. There's a moment's awkward silence.

"So, are you going to go home for a bit? Spend some time with your parents? I'm sure your course tutor would be okay with it."

"They'd probably be fine with it, but I wouldn't. I don't always get on with my dad, and my mum's not with us any more. Cancer." It's easier to pre-empt the curiosity and get it over with.

It must be a fraction warmer outside than yesterday, as it's now raining almost horizontally. We timed it well in theory, but my desire to escape this bloody awful conversation is impeded by the dismal weather. I frantically search my mind for something to say. Becky's brilliant at this sort of stuff. She always seems to know what to say and when. Sanjay is pretty cool about it too. I'm hopeless.

"What about your family?" I ask finally.

"None left. It's not a problem though. I have a different kind of family now." He gives a grim smile, but encouraging enough for me to ask some more.

"What do you mean?"

"I have a group of friends and, well, followers I suppose, who come to spend time in my house and learn from me. I think I mentioned my workshops at the ball."

"Yes. I'd quite like to try one, but I'm not sure now's the

right time."

"Do you remember me telling you that I'm a Kabbalist – a teacher of Kabbalah? You know what that is, don't you?"

"Jewish mysticism, isn't it? I thought you had to be over forty to start learning it. I'm sure I heard that somewhere. Oh, and haven't you got to know the Torah forwards, backwards and inside out as well?"

"All myths, Dan. Some of the rabbis wanted to keep the secrets to themselves, so they made out there were really dangerous secrets within Kabbalah. Anyone interested can learn though. They say even Madonna is interested and follows some of the teachings." He grins at me, and I start to relax a bit.

"What sort of people do you teach?"

"All sorts. Students, mums, dads – ordinary Jews who are interested in getting closer to Hashem."

"Hashem?"

"Did you not go to Hebrew classes?" he says.

"When I was coming up to Bar Mitzvah. Other than that, no. Hang on, Hashem is God, isn't that right?"

"We try not to say the name. It's one of the Ten Commandments." He looks intently at me, and I feel my ears grow warm. How could I be so stupid?

"Hey, it's okay. If you've not been to Hebrew classes, and I guess you didn't go to a Jewish school, how would you be expected to know this stuff? Anyway, I gather some people interpret that Commandment as 'don't swear', but that's not what it means."

"Okay. Thanks. And no. My family isn't religious at all. The closest I got after my Bar Mitzvah was to go to the youth club. And that was far more about socialising than the religion itself."

"Fair enough. Anyway, Dan, you don't have to be religious to be interested in Kabbalah. You just need to have an open mind and a searching soul. And a time of grief can be a good time to search."

"Maybe." My usual disinclination for discussing personal things with strangers takes over. "Look, Alan, I'm really sorry, but I think my concussion is getting to me a bit. I'm getting a blinding headache. Maybe cider wasn't a great idea."

"Sorry, mate, I should have thought. The rain's easing up a bit. Shall we make a dash for it, and get you back to your room?"

"Sure, thanks." I get my jacket on while he has another mouthful of beer.

"Aren't you driving?" I ask. "You said you live in North Manchester?"

"Yes on both counts, but I'll be fine on one pint. Although I might grab something to eat down here so that it soaks it up a bit before I head home."

We head out into the rain. It has lightened up a bit, but we're still pretty wet by the time we get back to the Tower. Whilst I'm not keen on inviting a man I don't know very well into my room, I can't let him head back out in this.

"Do you want to come up and dry off a bit?" I ask when we're in the foyer on the ground floor.

"No, it's fine. Why don't you come up to the house on Friday though? I'm hosting for Shabbat. You can meet some of my Kabbalists. They're lovely, you'll be made very welcome, and you can stay over until the end of Shabbat. One of the lads who joins us regularly is a student over in Oak House. I'll let him know to come for you at about three. He's got a car. You'll just about get to us in time before sundown."

"Okay, if you're sure. What's his name?"

"Simon. He's a nice guy. I'll get him to knock on for you Friday at three then. See you. Look after yourself."

"Thanks. You too."

A minute later he's gone, and I'm in a crowded lift heading back upstairs. I have no idea why I agreed to go to Alan's house for dinner and meet all his 'followers'. It's very strange. Somehow, I didn't feel able to say no.

Chapter Nine
Thursday 26/1/89

Becky

I avoid Rick's parents this morning and go to lectures instead. I don't think I could face them, even though all I've removed are some very private letters and a packet of condoms. What do you say to people whose nineteen-year-old son is suddenly dead? Particularly when no one knows if he killed himself?

I confess I read the letters through in detail when I got back to my room yesterday. I was a bit shocked by the explicit language and ideas expressed in the correspondence. I can't even bring myself to quote bits. This squeamishness on my part is quite pathetic, but if this falls into the wrong hands…

The important fact, though, is that there was no suggestion of a love affair – no emotion expressed other than lust. No hint that Rick was in love with Joanna, or vice versa. There were eight letters in total, all similar in tone: gritty, coarse and repellent. Obviously I'm only seeing her side of the conversation, but comments made by her suggest a mutual lack of affection. Passion, if it can be called that, was entirely superficial.

I threw the letters into a drawer last night in disgust. They were making me feel queasy, with her descriptions of bondage, self-torture and mention of the resultant pain in a way that suggested it turned her on. She seemed to expect it to turn Rick on as well. Maybe that was why he kept them.

Returning to my room after lectures, I take the letters out of my drawer once more. I'd like to burn them, but I don't dare. Taking them to the police seems to be the correct procedure, and I'm putting them into a carrier bag in preparation when I notice another letter, stuffed into the envelope of one I've already read. It's smaller, folded tightly and tucked in. I'm not sure how I missed it last night.

I take it out with reluctance. It's probably more of the same. I wrinkle my nose, and start reading…

14th January 1989
Well Rick, I think it has to be over. We've had fun, you and I, living out our fantasies on paper, but reality gets in the way. I wish we could have done half this stuff. The other half – maybe not.

Dad died yesterday, and that fucking bitch came into my room this morning to say she's throwing me out. I have to leave my home, where I've lived all my life, and get a job, so she can have the fucking house to herself. Like I said, reality sucks.

Thanks for everything, and I mean everything!
Joanna

Poor Joanna. So maybe it was all a game to her before. And then life upped and got in the way. But is any of this relevant to the case?

What am I like? Case! Like I'm a proper detective! I don't think I can leave it up to Bannister and his pals though. They seemed a bit pathetic and not very interested. I've got a vested interest, in that if I can solve this, it might help Dan.

I know I need to turn the letters over to the police, but I can't help thinking they may contain clues – if only this last letter. I should probably hand in the cake-crumbed foil as well, just in case. My eyes alight on the camera on my desk. I've not changed the film yet, and I need to get the roll developed with all the photos of Rick's room. I carefully rewind the camera to put all the film inside the lightproof canister before I open the back and swap it for a new film.

I rummage in the desk drawer and retrieve a coloured envelope from amongst the sundry leaflets, letters and torn-out news articles. It's labelled *Truprint*, and I dither between sending the film off or taking it into town and getting the photos developed there. I put the canister in the envelope for safe keeping anyway and put it into my Uni rucksack. It's now three o'clock, and if I get a bus I can scoot to the police station and hand in the letters. But first I photograph the last letter, the envelopes, front and back, and a sample of the remaining letters. I'd do them all, but I'm running out of film. There's no suggestion of a first letter, so perhaps that was either thrown away or received when Rick was home.

On the bus a short while later, I weigh up the significance of the letters. Where is Joanna now? Is she safe? I can't help feeling sorry for her, however repulsive the correspondence. It must be horrendous to be thrown out of her home following the death of a parent.

Longsight Police Station is a long, wet walk from the bus stop, and I'm feeling grumpy by the time I shiver my way in through the front doors. I go to the reception desk.

"Is DI Bannister here?" I ask through chattering teeth.

"Not now, love, he's off duty – finished at three." The uniformed officer behind the desk gives me a pitying look. "Anything I can help you with?"

The reception area is empty apart from us. I seem to have timed it well, apart from the rain.

"Yes please. I'm Becky White. I've come about the death of Rick Kennedy. I was asked by the house tutor to go through his things and pack them up for his parents – Rick's parents, that is. Anyway, I found these letters in his suitcase. I don't know if they're relevant, but would you be able to give them to DI Bannister?" I finish with another shiver. I really can't seem to warm up now.

"DS Lucas is here. She's assisting the inspector with this case. Would you like to chat to her? I think one of the interview rooms is available, and I might be able to rustle you up a brew." He finishes with a friendly wink, and I'm sold. I've been in Manchester long enough now to know that a brew is a cup of tea, and it's just what I need. I'm also curious to meet the lady Sergeant. I've always fancied becoming a detective, but Dad keeps saying it's not the career for a nice Jewish girl. Rats! The truth is he wants me and Ian to join the family law firm.

Five minutes later, I'm in a dingy interview room with my coat dripping from a peg behind the door, awaiting the arrival of DS Lucas. A steaming mug of tea is in front of me, and I wrap my hands around it. I glance around the room. There's a table and four chairs. Other than that, the peg, and some recording equipment on the table, the room is empty. There are no windows. I shiver again, but I'm not sure how much this time is from the cold, and how much is from the knowledge of the number of criminals that have sat in this very chair. A sobering thought. Especially since I don't think I've done anything wrong, although perhaps going through the letters might have been beyond my remit.

The door opens, and a tall brown-haired woman of maybe thirty comes into the room with a warm smile.

"Becky White?"

"Yes, that's me."

"I'm Wendy Lucas, Sergeant on the Rick Kennedy case. How can I help?"

I explain about the letters, and the foil, then have a sip of tea. The hot liquid sears through me, seeming to warm every cell in my body.

"Do you have them with you?" asks the Sergeant.

"Yes of course. Sorry." I extract the carrier bag from my rucksack and hand it over to her.

"I don't suppose you handled them with gloves?"

"Sorry. I didn't expect to find anything of any importance when I was packing up his stuff. I guess I assumed the forensics people will have checked everything." I spread out my hands. "You can take my fingerprints if that would help?"

She gives me an amused look, but it's not unfriendly. "Maybe later. Let's have a chat first."

I nod, intrigued. "Okay."

"Drink your tea, you still look a bit chilled. So, why did you get picked to clear out Rick's room?"

The tea-drinking gives me a moment to think, but DS

Lucas doesn't seem to have a hidden agenda, and could be useful later on, so I decide to be honest with her, although I may not reveal everything.

"Martin – that's our house tutor – feels able to talk to me. He usually seems to get flustered by girls. From what he said, I gathered the police had asked him questions about Rick, and he was embarrassed at not knowing the answers."

"Why didn't he ask one of the boys then?"

"I think he wanted the female perspective. For a lot of girls, Rick was like a honey pot to bees. He had looks, charm, and a kind of lazy arrogance that seemed to appeal to a lot of the girls in Halls."

"Not to you?"

"No." My answer feels too abrupt and the officer sits waiting for more. "There's another guy I like. I don't seem to have the emotional capacity to focus on more than one at a time."

"That's not a bad trait, Becky. Don't knock it." She grins. "There's a lot of crime caused by people's predilections for focussing on several partners at once."

"I suppose so. Crimes of passion."

"Yeah. So who is he?"

"Daniel. He was good friends with Rick." Shit. I hadn't meant to bring Dan into it. She somehow got the question in when I wasn't watching.

"Tell me about Daniel." DS Lucas sits back in her chair, looking relaxed and friendly. She takes a sip from the mug she brought in with her – coffee judging by the smell. There's nothing in her demeanour to make me wary, but I'm anxious to protect my friend, and I'm on my guard now. This woman is like a cat rolling on its back, pretending to be submissive, whilst constantly ready to pounce. I'm a little in awe of her tactics, and respect her for it. But I'm still not going to feed Dan to her.

"He's a lovely guy. Quiet, a bit shy, but with a great sense of humour. We were friends through our youth club before we came to Uni. I've known him a couple of years."

"Okay, what about you? Tell me a bit about yourself."

Relieved that she's moved topic, I relax again.

"What do you want to know? I'm eighteen; I come from near Radlett in Hertfordshire, and I'm studying Law."

"What do you want to do when you finish? Solicitor, barrister…?"

I feel myself going red, and I look down at the table for a moment. Then grabbing courage with both hands, I look directly at her. "I want to go into the police force. I've wanted to be a detective for as long as I can remember. Law seemed like a good starting point, and a way to shut my dad up. He doesn't think a career as a detective is a good one." No need to mention the family business just now.

To give the Sergeant credit, she looks straight back at me, a serious expression on her face.

"It can be tough as a detective in the police. Women have to work even harder to get anywhere. You wouldn't think it nowadays, when it's just as easy to get a degree if you're a woman, but as soon as you get into the workplace, attitudes are still… let's say, old-fashioned. So, it's not easy. But if you want it, and you're prepared to put in the crazy hours, and learn when to speak up, and when to shut up, it can be rewarding. For what it's worth, Becky, I think you'd make a good detective."

"Thanks." A kaleidoscope of feelings are swishing around in me at the moment, and I'm unsure what else to say.

She grins mischievously. "So now we've established your career aspirations, I don't need to ask whether you opened the letters. Perhaps we can just discuss what you found out?"

Ouch. I walked into that. I give her a brief description of the contents of most of the letters, trying to convey the crudeness without resorting to quotation.

"It's the last letter that's interesting though." I watch as DS Lucas gets some gloves from her pocket and empties the carrier bag on to the table. I flush again. I should have used gloves, but I didn't have any on me. I point at the envelope with the final letter stuffed in the back. "That one, Sergeant. There are two letters in there, with different dates. It's the one that's folded up quite small."

"Call me Wendy," she says, opening up the sheet of paper. She reads it quickly, her eyes scanning the words before looking back at me. "Yes, I see what you mean." Removing the other sheet from the same envelope, she scans that one as well. "Interesting contrast." She lays them out on the desk. "What do you see?"

I glance at her, startled, but return my gaze to the papers in front of me.

"Same pen. Handwriting looks a bit different. Could that be the distress of hearing that her dad had died and she was going to be thrown out?"

"Possibly. I think it could have been written by two different people though. I'll pass it on to the analysts, and see what they can find out. But it certainly raises interesting questions. Thanks for bringing them in, Becky. I'll definitely follow up on this." Wendy returns the letters to the plastic bag and stands up. I follow suit. It seems the interview is at an end. She puts her hand on my shoulder as she ushers me to the door, then stops and faces me.

"Promise me you'll be careful. Tell your friend Daniel to watch his back too. We don't know yet if Rick's death was by his own hand, but if it wasn't, there's someone out there with a nasty secret, and he or she could prove very dangerous."

"Do you mind me asking, what was the cause of death?"

"Barbiturates overdose. There was a syringe on the desk in his room, containing traces, and lethal amounts were found in his system. There was no label on the vial that was next to the syringe, suggesting it wasn't his prescription, and his doctor confirmed they hadn't been prescribed by him." Wendy looks at me, clearly awaiting my thoughts.

"So, either he got it from someone else, or…"

"Precisely. Or! That's why I want you and Daniel to be careful. If Rick did obtain the vial from someone else, it suggests there was a definite attempt to take his own life. Only an idiot would inject to help them sleep. None of our information about Rick suggests he was an idiot."

Wendy looks at her watch, then thanks me for bringing the letters, and turfs me back out into the cold. I return to Halls, and try to concentrate on an essay, but all I can think about is someone entering Rick's room, and stabbing him with a syringe full of a lethal dose of drugs.

How did the killer get in? Did Rick let them in? Or was he really stupid enough, or desperate enough to take the drugs himself?

Chapter Ten
Friday 27/1/89

Daniel

I get through the next two days on autopilot. I manage somehow to dress and clean my teeth. Becky drags me to meals and glares at me until I eat. I want to tell her about the impending Shabbat visit to Alan's group, but my tongue seems to stick to the roof of my mouth whenever I think about mentioning it.

I haven't made it into lectures yet. I wrote a letter to my tutor explaining that my best friend just died, and I don't feel able to come in yet. Becky's friend Amy took it in. She's on my course, but not in my tutor group. I don't know her very well, considering we're doing the same thing, but she seems okay, and has offered to copy out her notes for me. Apparently, the more times she writes them, the better she remembers. It's never quite worked like that for me, but I guess everyone's different.

So between meals, I lie on my bed and stare at the ceiling. I tried music. A cassette tape. But it was one that Rick had put together for me. I managed to get through one song before turning it off, but an hour later I was still sobbing. That was Wednesday night. Silence has filled the room since then.

It's Friday afternoon now. Two o'clock. I can't remember the name of the chap who's going to take me to Alan's. He lives in Oak House, but I don't know which flat. The only way I could cancel would be to phone Alan, or to just turn the guy away when he turns up. I don't even know if I want to turn him away. Maybe it would do me good to get out of this bloody room. And maybe to get out of my head, even if only for a little while. The headache I got on Wednesday after one pint of cider put me off wanting to get drunk. I reckon I've still got a bit of concussion. Alcohol is not the answer for the moment. So the only way to escape my head is company. And perhaps the company of strangers.

I don't know what the hell I want. I clasp my hands behind my head, and catch a whiff of armpit. Shit. I need a shower. The dressing is still on my head, but I'll have to improvise.

Half an hour later, the smell has been dramatically improved, thanks to sitting up in a bubbly bath and having a good wash. I even managed to wash what little hair the doctor left me with. The dressing got a bit damp but nothing too bad. It'll dry. Deodorant and after-shave finish the job. I'm clean and I smell okay.

Unbelievably, there's a clean shirt in the wardrobe. I have three decent shirts, and two are in the washing basket. This is my least favourite – dark blue with grey spots – but it goes with jeans. It'll have to do.

I feel a bit better for being clean, but there's still a really obvious white bandage on the back of my head. Without a hoodie, I can't easily cover it up. All my hoodies stink. I'm dithering, when there's a knock.

Bloody hell. It's three o'clock on the dot. I open the door. The young man standing in the corridor is about the same age as me, but he's about six foot tall. I take in the spotless black trousers, white shirt and thin black tie, with inward horror. I've not even got a tie here.

"Hi, I'm Simon. We need to get going. Have you got a yarmulke?" He seems pleasant, but slightly impatient.

I extract my one and only kippah from my top drawer. It's blue with silver trim, and looks a bit dated next to his plain black one. I've got used to the different names people use for these items. Where I live, we call them kippahs, but I've since heard koppel and yarmulke. Non-Jewish folk call them skull caps. I hold it up briefly to show him then shove it into my jeans pocket.

"Yeah sure." I grab my jacket, key and wallet and follow Simon back to the lifts. "You're very punctual. What happened to JMT?"

"What? Oh, Jewish Mean Time! That doesn't work very well when you've got to beat the Manchester traffic to get to north side before Shabbat kicks in."

He doesn't speak again until we get outside. "They let me bring the car into the car park here when I promised it was only for a few minutes, so we'd better get cracking."

He leads me to a battered green Vauxhall Nova. As different as possible from Alan's shiny black car. It's neat and clean inside though.

"Thanks for agreeing to take me to Alan's. It's nice of you when you've never met me."

"Alan's a top guy. If he asks a favour, it's the thing to do to say yes." Simon keeps his eyes on the road at all times, negotiating the heavy Friday traffic with steadiness and skill. His tone is cold though. I don't know if he doesn't like me or if it's natural reserve. I settle into silence for a while, but by the time we get to the city centre, it's becoming ominous. I rub my sweaty palms onto my jeans. I've come out without a hankie in the rush, and I don't feel inclined to ask the driver.

I take a deep breath.

"So, what's the plan for tonight?"

"Did Alan not tell you?" Contempt fills the confined space of the car. I wish I hadn't asked. I'll find out soon enough, but going into strange situations alone is not my favourite occupation. And with the attitude of the guy next to me, I might as well be alone. I grit my teeth.

"He just said to come for dinner and meet some people."

"Well, that's more or less it. Did he mention about staying to the end of Shabbat?"

"Shit. I forgot about that bit. I've not got anything with me." I look out of the window. We're driving past the Arndale Shopping Centre, but parking isn't an option, and time is moving on.

"You'll have to make do. Alan has a few spares of pyjamas and stuff for people who get stranded over Shabbat. You'll survive."

This trip is not going well. The gnawing in my stomach

has little to do with the fact that I've not eaten since breakfast. Becky was in lectures most of today so I didn't bother with lunch. My hands are sweaty again, but I don't want to show this jerk that he's getting to me, so I rest my palms on my thighs, and try to dry them without drawing his attention.

The next twenty minutes pass in awkward silence. Simon is clearly not going to be a friend. Hopefully the rest of Alan's followers will be easier to chat to. Otherwise I'd have been better staying in my room.

Tension builds as we head from the city centre into the suburban districts of North Manchester. By the time the car pulls up outside a large house, I feel sick and my head is throbbing. Simon turns the engine off, and I gaze out of the window as a group of religious men in large hats walk past.

"We're here. Let's get inside. Alan'll be waiting for us. We're just in time. Shabbat starts in five minutes."

Chapter Eleven
Friday 27/1/89

Becky

The day starts badly. I miss a bus by seconds. The next bus doesn't bother stopping, but accelerates through a huge puddle next to the bus stop. Soaked through, I give serious thought to going back to my room to get changed, but I can see a double-decker in the distance, and if I don't get on it, I'll be late for my tutorial. Cold and wet, I clamber on to the bus a moment later and take a seat next to a pregnant woman near the front. We exchange smiles, but then she focuses on the novel she has in her hands.

I turn my thoughts to the impending session with my tutor. He's been reviewing a couple of essays I handed in. They feel trivial and irrelevant after what's happened this week. Both essays were written while Rick was alive and well, and presumably exchanging sexy letters with Joanna.

I manage to dry off a bit on the bus, but it's pointless, as the two-minute run from the bus stop into Uni is long enough for me to get drenched again. By the time I arrive at my tutor's door, I'm soggy, bedraggled and out of breath.

"Come in, Miss White. You're late." Dr Leeson always addresses us formally. He says it's to prepare us for a career in law, but I suspect it's because it's easier to inject sarcasm into a title and surname. "Or would you prefer to go to the bathrooms to dry off, and keep everyone waiting a while longer?" The other three members of the tutor group look steadily at the floor, although Justine flashes me a quick glance of sympathy first.

"Sorry, Sir." The idiot tells us he expects to be addressed

as Sir. I reckon it suits his ego – mild compensation for not reaching the status of Barrister or the dizzying heights of Judge. I sit down hurriedly on the empty plastic chair.

I have a few minutes to recover my composure as he tears into Justine, ripping her essay to shreds – not literally, thank goodness. Then he turns to me.

"So, Miss White, not only do you arrive late today, but last week you presented me with an essay that a four-year-old could have written better."

Can four-year-olds write two thousand words on the subject of Property Law and Trusts? I doubt it. They have better things to do. And so do I.

I stay silent, and allow him to continue his rant, which he does with eloquence and asperity. His quotes make it sound worse than it actually is, although this aspect of law is not my forte. My thoughts drift back to Rick and to the police station, wondering what the Sergeant is doing with Joanna's letters.

"Miss White, are you paying attention?" The incredulity in Leeson's voice would be funny if it wasn't so scary.

"Sorry Sir, yes of course." He'd better not ask what he just said.

He doesn't. Instead, he turns the essay sideways, and rips it in half. Literally. Bastard!

He lets the pieces fall to the floor. "One more attempt, Miss White, to be here on my desk by nine-fifteen on Monday morning." His face is inches from my own, and I can smell the bacon he had for breakfast. I try not to retch. "Do you understand me, Miss White?"

I nod and attempt to back away, but there's nowhere to go. The chair is against the wall. After a long moment, he stands up straight again. The rest of the tutorial is focussed on others in the group, but as we file out at the end, he calls me back.

"A few seconds of your precious time, Miss White." It's a demand rather than a request, and I turn to face him. "You may find this reading list useful. If your updated essay is not a significant improvement, I'll have you thrown off the course." His face is in front of mine again, and my stomach clenches in response to a sudden fear of this man – a tutor who up until now inspired only contempt.

The day improves slightly, as I don't have to see Leeson again, but the rest of it consists of a set of boring lectures, punctuated with brief jolts as I see or hear things that remind me of Rick: a student that wears a similar shirt to one he regularly wore; posters on the noticeboard about the Samaritans. Did Rick commit suicide? I spend a lot of time pondering this during the lectures, but fail to come to a conclusion other than that it seems unlikely. I need more evidence.

I debate returning to the police station when I've finished, but I was only there yesterday and I don't want to hassle too much. Finally, at four o'clock, it's time to head back to Halls. I check my purse, but it's empty apart from a few coppers. Damn! I've left my cash card on my desk in my room. I can't even remember why I took it out, but it's no good there. I don't have enough cash on me to get the bus. I'll have to walk back. And it's still throwing it down. I try to mentally prepare myself to get very wet, but it just makes me miserable.

The walk seems interminable, but I try to distract myself by thinking of my dreaded essay and what I need to do to improve it over the weekend. So I barely notice what's going on around me. It's one straight road from Uni to Halls, so I don't need to think about where I'm going. Suddenly, I'm grabbed and dragged into an alley.

"What…?" A hand is clamped over my mouth before I can ask what's going on. I wish I'd started to scream, but it's too late now. I can see three youths in hooded tops and baseball caps. The tallest is standing directly in front of me. There's a fourth – a strong thug who I can't see, but whose arm is half-strangling me. His other hand is over my mouth. Forced to breathe through my nose, I'm struck by the overpowering stench: the stale cigarette smoke that clings to their clothes, and the spirits on their breath. Panic fills my body, and I can't think what to do. Fight or flight? Neither seems like an option.

"Pretty fing, ain't you? Apart from the conk, but that's not your fault. We'll enjoy you, love." The tall guy in front of me extracts a knife and flashes it in front of me. I feel it nick my cheek. And then he shows it to me; a vicious-looking blade, several inches long. "You gonna spread your legs here, or wait until we get you back to our pad?"

Have I got a choice? How about not at all? The strong guy still has his grip on me. My arms are free though. It's now or never. My right hand is close to my coat pocket. With a swift motion, I locate a device I was given at the beginning of term and press the ends together.

An ear-splitting siren sound is emitted. I'm nearly deafened myself, but I hear one of the boys mutter "Fucking bitch!" The guy holding me lets go, and I run. My feet take me faster than I've ever run before, and I don't stop until I'm back in Halls about ten minutes later, panting and terrified, but thanking God, and the Students' Union for providing me with a rape alarm.

I step out of the lift on the tenth floor. I can't face my own company just now. I turn right down the boys' corridor and knock on Daniel's door.

Chapter Twelve
Friday 27/1/89

Daniel

Alan welcomes me into a large room – a lounge of sorts, filled with a couple of sofas, armchairs and several dining chairs. None of them match. All are occupied. I'm suddenly conscious of being a complete stranger with a large white dressing on the back of my head. I feel horribly conspicuous and am aware of turning scarlet. Everyone stops talking as I enter, and they turn to stare at me.

"Friends," says Alan in a loud voice, "meet Daniel. He's come to join us this Shabbat, and hopefully for many more."

There's a murmur of greetings, but when I dare to look up, the looks are almost hostile. I don't understand why, but I wish I could get out of here. I glance at my host, and Alan gives me a reassuring smile.

"You'll be fine, Dan," he whispers in my ear.

"Alan, are we getting started soon? Now that your new friend has arrived?" The speaker is a large brown-haired woman in her forties or fifties. Her lips are full and pouty, and she reminds me of a sulky child.

Alan nods at her. "Short service first, then dinner. Won't be long now." He waves towards an empty folding chair that's lurking behind a large pot plant. I hadn't noticed that one. I negotiate my way past a tangle of legs and curious stares, and plonk myself on the chair, grateful for its more obscure location.

"Are we ready to start, ladies and gents?" Alan looks pointedly at me, and I flush with embarrassment and confusion.

"Yarmulke on, dozy sod," Simon hisses at me.

Mortified now, I fish in my pocket and get the kippah on my head.

The service begins. It's all standard stuff – a typical Friday night service similar to those from youth group weekends. I switch off after a few minutes; the words are ingrained into me, so I don't need to concentrate. I focus instead on the group of people around me. Ages range from about my age up to maybe mid-sixties. I count fifteen in total, including myself and Alan. Most of them have made it obvious they would rather I was not here, but as I allow my gaze to wander around the room, I notice a young woman looking anxiously at me. I give her a half-smile, and she smiles back. She's youngish, maybe in her twenties, and pleasant-looking, with straight dark brown hair falling to her waist, and dark eyes. She's sitting a few feet away from me, and there are a couple of more hostile people in between, but I feel infinitely better for the sight of a friendly face.

When the service ends, she comes straight over to me.

"Hi, I'm Rachel. Daniel, isn't it?" She holds her hand out and I shake it.

"Hi Rachel. Nice to meet you. Please call me Dan. Most of my friends do." I look around again. People are generally chatting amongst themselves, and are ignoring me. But that's fine. I only need one ally.

"Sit next to me at dinner, Dan. It's quite daunting when you don't know anyone, and they can be quite cliquey here." Her voice is low, but Simon is standing nearby and seems to overhear. He shoots Rachel a filthy look, which she doesn't seem to notice.

Alan comes over to join us. His suit and tie are immaculate, but his hand goes to the tie knot and he drags it downwards.

"Now the service is over, I can take this thing off. I have to wear it for work, and it seems appropriate to wear for leading services, but I hate ties." He grins at Rachel, then turns to me. "How are you doing, Dan? Difficult crowd here tonight. It varies, but some weekends are a bit more laid-back than others, if you know what I mean."

"That's true," says Rachel. "He's right, Dan. There are some lovely people in the group. They're obviously tied up this weekend. Shame."

"Are you staying over, Rache?" Alan asks. There's a certain something in his voice, coupled perhaps with the abbreviated name, that alerts me. I glance at her. She blushes.

"Not tonight. My dad's walking round at eleven to pick me up. He decided it's not appropriate for his twenty-five-year-old unmarried daughter to sleep over at the house of a bachelor, even when there are a load of other people staying. I'll walk back in the morning. I'm only half a mile away."

Alan looks a bit disappointed, and he's not the only one. I'm not impressed with anyone here except for Rachel. Obviously Alan's nice, but he's going to be in demand.

As we head for the huge dining table in the next room, Rachel stays at my side, and manages to get a seat next to me. Although I suspect that even if she'd followed several minutes behind, she'd have still been able to sit next to me. Everyone else seems anxious to avoid me. I don't know why.

"You'll be fine without me tonight," she says in a low voice when we're seated. "It usually finishes before eleven, so you could go straight to bed. I'll be here in time for breakfast."

I smile gratefully at her. It's a huge relief to find someone who understands, even though she barely knows me. She returns the smile, but as I turn to accept some challah, I notice her nodding to Alan. Has she agreed to help him out by being friendly? I break into the sweet bread but wait for the prayer before eating it.

The meal is tasty and plentiful, and must have cost a fortune to get this catered. I assume the chickens are kosher for a gathering like this. It's a traditional Friday night meal of chicken soup, roast chicken and dessert – dairy-free ice-cream in this case.

Rachel chatters to me throughout the meal, telling me about her job as a secretary to the boss of a big local firm of solicitors. I make a mental note to tell Becky, in case she needs to do some work experience as part of her course.

It's pleasant to listen to her speak; I don't have to think too much. She's not asking me anything personal. I'm finally quite relaxed. It's been three days now since I hit my head, so I've risked a couple of glasses of wine, and it's been okay. No major banging headache yet.

I'm conscious that ugly thoughts and feelings are only a short step below the surface, but I seem able to keep them at bay for the moment.

Dinner is finished at nine-thirty. Another hour and a half to go. Suddenly my insides have a wobble, and I feel a bit queasy. What's coming next?

Alan stands up and taps a spoon against a glass. When everyone falls quiet, he says, "Thanks folks. Give me five minutes to rearrange the lounge, then come in. Daniel and Rachel, can you give me a hand please?"

We both stand and go through to the room where the prayer service was held.

"Do you want the chairs in a circle, Alan?" Rachel asks.

"Yes, please. Leave the sofas where they are. We can work around them." He turns to me. "We usually sit in a circle after dinner and discuss ways we can get closer to Hashem. It's very therapeutic."

Bloody hell. That's not my idea of therapy. It sounds terrifying. I feel a bit lightheaded at the thought.

"You'll be fine." Rachel puts down the chair she's holding, and rests a hand on my shoulder. "You don't have to say much tonight, as it's your first time. But it will be good for you to hear what others have to say."

"Yeah, sure." I force myself to smile at her and pull myself together enough to help with rearranging the furniture. I glance at Alan. He seems absorbed, and I don't like to ask anything. My stomach is in knots and I wish I could leave.

As we're finishing up, the others drift into the room in twos and threes. Rachel pulls me to a chair next to her, and I sit down, a little relieved at not being abandoned. As soon as everyone is seated, Alan gets everyone's attention again with the spoon and glass.

"Okay, everyone. You know the format. Obviously, we've got a newcomer today, so I'll just give a quick rundown for Daniel." My face grows warm with embarrassment as he speaks directly to me. "As you don't know anyone, we'll go around the circle, and each person will say their name, and an item of interest about themselves, before sharing what they've done this week to find Hashem. Then we'll open up the discussion for everyone to join in and discuss how we can do better next week. When we meet up next Shabbat, we'll all be able to see if our goals have been met, or if we've at least got closer to achieving them."

I nod, but I'm torn between feeling as if this is a load of bullshit, and being terrified about what to say when it's my go. Despite Rachel's reassurance, I have a horrible feeling that I'll be expected to say something. Anger and grief are not a pathway to Hashem in my view, so I think I'm going to fail at this spectacularly.

I try to take in names at least as the evening progresses, but remember just a few: Anthony, a man in his thirties who has been to shul every night this week, but not managed to read or understand the Hebrew; Cara, a woman of around forty who has spent extra time with her family this week, making sure she put the children to bed, rather than leaving it to her husband (I do wonder why she's abandoned them for Shabbat, but who am I to talk?); and Sarah, the woman who was rude to me at the beginning of the evening, has been to something called a mikvah – apparently a special bath – and cleansed herself after her monthly period before resuming relations with her husband. I'm not entirely sure why she wants to own up to this in front of a lot of strangers. It's a bit too much information for me.

They're all admirable things from a Judaism perspective, but I'm not sure they quite get it. Not sure I get it either, but isn't this process about feeling closer to God? I reserve judgement for the moment, as Rachel is speaking about her own efforts to learn Hebrew, and I'm up next.

Suddenly everyone is glaring at me. I feel as though I'm drowning in a sea of hostile, unfamiliar faces, and it's time to sink or swim.

I blurt out, "I'm Daniel. This week my best friend was found dead. I feel like shit. And don't fucking tell me there's any way out of this to get closer to 'Hashem', cos it all sounds like a load of fucking bullshit." I stand up, wriggle between chairs to leave the circle, and leg it out of the room, and out of the front door, slamming it behind me. I rest my back against the wall, and swear profusely for several minutes before sinking to the ground, and resting my head in my hands.

That was such a bloody stupid thing to do. Alan at least has shown me nothing but kindness, and I've just shoved it down his throat. I'm such a prick.

The door opens and I look up. Rachel's standing there. She pauses and fiddles with the latch.

"I'd better make sure we don't get locked out. They're carrying on without us for the moment. Alan knows I'm out here with you, but the others haven't realised." She comes and squats down next to me. "I'm sorry, I hadn't realised what you've been through this week. I can't actually believe Alan brought you here so soon. Another couple of weeks' time might have been more appropriate."

"Yeah maybe, but I was going crazy staring at the walls of my bedroom and wondering if it was my fault."

It starts raining, that horrible icy kind of rain that Manchester seems to produce at this time of year.

"We'd better get inside, or we'll freeze." Rachel stands up and reaches out a hand to me. I take it and she pulls me to my feet. "Come on, we can go and talk in the dining room."

I follow her into the room where we had dinner. It's a bit of a mess, and I'm now reluctant to get into a deep conversation with someone I've only just met. I suggest we clear up a bit.

"Good idea. Alan usually does it after everyone's gone home or to bed, so we'll save him a job."

I hadn't particularly noticed earlier, but all the plates are disposable. Even the cutlery is an expensive sort of plastic: gold-coloured, and more solid than the usual throwaway knives and forks, but disposable none the less.

It only takes us about ten minutes to empty all the rubbish into a black bin liner, and take condiments and bottles of wine and soda into the kitchen. When there's nothing left on the table but the still-burning Shabbat candles, I resign myself to a long chat. It's not even ten-thirty yet, and Rachel's dad is due at eleven. There's no escape.

Chapter Thirteen
Friday 27/1/89

Becky

Unable to find Daniel, I go to my room. My hands shake as I fumble with the door key. I wade through the mess on the floor to get to my bed, and sit on the mattress with my back against the wall, and my arms around my knees.

My breathing has returned to near normal, but shivers take over my body. I'm not sure if I'm cold or just in shock, but now the immediate danger is gone, I feel extremely unwell. *Should I get help?* Nothing actually happened, thank God, but I was lucky. What if the next girl doesn't have an alarm, or doesn't manage to get to it?

I have a business card that DS Wendy Lucas gave me. I dig it out of my purse, together with a handful of coins, and drag myself to the door. My limbs are heavy and aching, as if I have flu, but I know I need to report this. I grab my keys and the rape alarm, and make sure my door is shut properly behind me. I seem to have got paranoid all of a sudden. There's no reason why anyone would wait for me in my room, but I check the door again anyway, pushing to make sure the lock has engaged.

When I get to the area by the lift, there's already a boy on the phone. I recognise Greg, and he gives me a quick grin, before focussing on me properly.

"Hey Dad, gotta go. Bit of an emergency. Speak to you later." He hangs up. "You're covered in blood, Becky, what happened? Wait, sit down. In fact, let's get you to the common room. Come on." He touches me gently on my shoulder, but I back off, panicking at even such a light touch.

"I'm sorry, Greg. I don't mean to offend you."

"I'm not offended, just concerned. What the hell has happened to you?" He indicates for me to go through the door into the common room, and I obey, almost collapsing into one of the fabric-covered chairs.

His kindness overwhelms me, and tears begin to flow. Greg passes me a white handkerchief.

"It's clean. Sorry it's a bit crumpled. Hold it against your cheek. I think that's where the blood's coming from." He pauses. "Are you okay here for two minutes? I've got something in my room that might help you?"

"I don't want to be here alone." It sounds so pathetic, but I still feel so scared. I clasp the hankie to my wet, sticky cheek.

"What happened, Becky? You've not told me yet. Is it something you can talk about? Anything I can help with?"

"I was attacked on the way home." I extract the rape alarm from my pocket with my free hand and show it to him. "There was a gang of lads – probably about our age, but not students." I stop to sniff. "They sounded like local lads. If I hadn't used this, I'd have been in real trouble." I have a quick look at the hankie. It's no longer white. "Sorry, Greg. I'll buy you a new one. If I can ever face going out again."

"Don't worry about it. I've got loads in my drawer. I've got an auntie that buys them for me every birthday and Christmas. No imagination, but they come in handy." He grins at me, then turns serious again. "I won't leave you here alone, but if anyone else comes in, we'll nab them, and I'll get you some brandy."

I'm about to say I don't need it, but I'm still shaking really badly, and struggle to get the alarm back into my pocket.

"I think I should tell the police. They might be able to stop them from hurting someone else. Will you come with me to the phone while I ring?"

"No, *you* come with *me* to the phone, while *I* ring. Whose card is that you're holding?"

I show him the card that I retrieved when I put the alarm away. "It's a Sergeant that I met when I went to talk to them about Rick. She's really nice."

"Come on. Keep that handkerchief against your face.

You're still bleeding." He takes my hand and helps me to my feet. This time the contact is more welcome.

There's someone on the phone when we get there, but Greg points to my bleeding face, and then to the phone. The girl apologises to whoever's on the other end and hangs up.

"Are you okay?" she asks.

I nod, and sit on the stairs while Greg makes the call. The girl hovers uncertainly for a moment, only leaving when I give her a tremulous smile. She's gone by the time the phone is answered.

"Hi. Can I speak to DS Lucas please? ... Yes, it's fairly urgent. A friend of mine has been attacked ... Becky White. ... Sure, I can hold a minute." He puts his hand over the receiver and looks at me. "He's just gone to get her." I nod and give him a half-smile. "Hello, is that DS Lucas? ... Yes of course. Becky, she wants to speak to you – is that okay?"

I drag myself off the stairs and take the receiver. "Hi, Becky here."

"Hi, it's Wendy Lucas. Are you okay?"

"Kind of. They didn't hurt me much, only cut my cheek. I'm just... just..." I can't say any more. Sobs catch in my throat, and I know if I say another word, I'll just blubber out loud.

"Right. Go and sit in the common room with someone you trust. Do you trust Greg? He seems like a nice lad."

"Yes," I sniff. The urge to sob my heart out subsides in the face of Wendy's calm practicality.

"Great, go and sit with him. I'll be with you in about twenty minutes. Now give me back to Greg, so I can get some details. I know which Halls you're in, but he can tell me exactly whereabouts. See you soon."

"Okay, thanks." I hand the phone over, and listen while Greg directs her to the tenth floor. When he puts the phone down, he helps me back to the comfy chairs in the common room. My legs have gone wobbly, and I don't mind his arm round my shoulders. We sit down in separate chairs though, to my relief. I'm still jumpy about too much contact.

"How was your day before this happened?" he says,

perhaps trying to pass the time.

"Oh bloody hell!"

"What? That bad?"

"I got an assignment returned. It's got to be completely rewritten this weekend. The tutor's a complete prick. He won't accept any excuses."

"Anything I can help with?"

"Do you know anything about Property Law and Trusts? It's got to be the most boring thing ever invented."

"No, not really. It does sound mind-numbingly dull. Maybe if you're feeling better tomorrow you might be able to concentrate on it. We can go to the library together if you want?"

"See how I feel tomorrow, but thanks." I ask him about his course, and a discussion of thermodynamics (of which I understand one word in four) tides us over until Wendy arrives.

I'm facing the door, so I see her as soon as she enters the room. She smiles and greets us, then fishes in her handbag, extracting a little first aid kit.

"Let's get you sorted out first, Becky. Greg, do you have brandy or rum? I think a spot of something like that would help."

Greg explains that he wanted to give me some but didn't want to leave me alone, then heads down the corridor towards his room.

"Great, once he comes back with the brandy, you and I can go along to your room and have a private chat. Does that sound alright?"

"Yes thanks. That would be better. He's nice, but…"

"Absolutely. We can get you properly cleaned up there as well."

Ten minutes later, I'm armed with a glass of brandy (I've promised to return the glass tomorrow) and am sitting on my bed telling Wendy everything. I have a dressing on my cheek and it's finally stopped bleeding.

"You did well to escape. I know that's probably not what

you want to hear, but most girls with a knife against their face wouldn't risk reaching for the rape alarm. Which reminds me..." She reaches into her handbag on the desk next to her, and extracts a new alarm. "I'll swap you. They're best only used once at full effect. It's okay to test them once in a while, but once you've used it for real, you should get a replacement. Here you go."

"Thanks. Maybe I should try a self-defence class. There's a judo group advertised on the Union notice board."

"That's sensible. I'd always recommend knowing how to defend yourself. So, you've told me about the attack. What do you remember about the attackers?"

I take a sip of brandy to fortify myself – I'd rather not think about it, let alone talk, but this might save another girl, so I have to try.

"There were at least four of them. The one who was behind me, half-strangling me, was a big guy – he felt strong, and when he put his hand over my mouth, his hand was kind of like a bunch of sausages – with big chunky fingers." I break off to let Wendy finish jotting in her notebook.

"Carry on. Do you remember anything else about him?" She pauses, and I shake my head. "How about the others then?"

"They were all white. I guess aged seventeen to early twenties. It's hard to say more accurately than that. They all reeked of tobacco and alcohol. The one who stood directly in front of me – he was the one with the knife – was over six foot tall. He was skinny, but looked kind of hard with it." I grimace. It's not easy to describe people I saw only once, and in a state of complete terror, but if I'm going to this, I need to do it properly. Wendy's sitting patiently and calmly on the chair in front of me, with her notebook held loosely in her hand. "You know how some skinny people look a bit wimpy? This lad looked as if he had the strength and mental cruelty to torture someone. There was this kind of evil joy in his eyes. Sorry that doesn't help much."

"Tell me about his eyes."

"It was getting a bit dark and the weather was awful, but

he was standing right in front of me. They were green, and close together. Kind of narrow and slitty, but I don't know if that was because of his expression. I didn't see the others as clearly. He was the tallest though – at least out of the ones in front of me. I don't think the guy strangling me was as tall. Just big. Of the others, the next tallest was maybe five foot ten. He was standing just a bit behind the slitty-eyed guy and was wearing a parka jacket with the hood up. Stocky build. Pale face. Stubby nose. I can't remember much else about him, but he seemed the next most intimidating."

"What about the other one?"

"He was a bit further back. Just a young lad – part of a gang. I don't know if he was a willing member who would join in with the violence given half a chance. Maybe it wasn't his turn, but I got the vague impression he was lower in the pecking order."

"Yes, probably. That tends to be how these gangs work. Do you remember anything else about them? You mentioned the next tallest wore a parka. What were the others wearing?" Wendy looks at me intently.

"The guy with the knife was wearing a grey hooded jumper with a leather jacket over the top. He had his hood up, so I couldn't see his hair, but from the little I saw at the very front, he seemed to have an almost shaved head. I think they all did, as far as I could tell. Not quite skinheads, but nearly."

"Thanks, Becky. You've done really well. If I was to get an identikit sorted, would you be willing to come in and help the artist do pictures of them?"

"I guess so. I suppose I remember more than I thought. Any idea when?"

"It will probably be Monday. Maybe when you've finished lectures, give me a call from the call box in the Students' Union. I'll either pick you up myself or send one of the WPCs."

"That would be great, thanks. To be honest, I'm a bit scared about travelling. I won't be walking again – ever."

"That's understandable, and sensible. It's about planning. Make sure you've got change for both bus fares before you leave here every morning. And when you're on the bus, if it's nearly empty, sit downstairs as near to the driver as you can."

"Yes of course. Thanks."

She gets up to leave, and pats me on the shoulder. "You'll be fine, Becky. It just takes a while to get over the shock. I'll see you Monday."

She shuts the door behind her, and I curl my arms round my knees. Now she's gone, the shakes return in full measure.

Chapter Fourteen
Saturday 28/1/89

Daniel

I'm woken by a loud knock on the door. I rub tired eyes. Sleep evaded me until the late into the night, and I can't have got more than a few hours. The combination of a sleeping bag on a sofa and borrowed nylon pyjamas after a stressful evening – it was never conducive to a restful night. The door knocker goes again. I check my watch. Seven-thirty. Yuk. It doesn't look like anyone else is getting up, so I drag myself out of the sleeping bag and pad to the door in my bare feet. The carpet in the hallway is worn, and cold seeps through from underneath. There's another loud knock just as I'm reaching for the latch.

"Hang on. I'm opening it." There's a chain across, and even in my sleep-deprived state, it occurs to me that the person outside might not be a friend. I leave it on, and open the door as far as the chain will allow.

"It's only me. Can I come in?" Rachel's standing there alone, getting drenched in the freezing rain.

"Sure." I close the door, release the chain, and open it properly to let her in. I'm slightly embarrassed at being seen in blue and white patterned pyjamas. "Do you want to make yourself a drink? I'll get myself dressed."

She nods, and ten minutes later I join her in the kitchen. The other occupants of the house are still apparently asleep, but they all had bedrooms, so they might be awake for all I know.

"There's hot water in the urn. Alan always sets it up before Shabbat comes in, so help yourself to tea or coffee."

"Thanks." I sort myself out with a cup of tea and sit down. There's an embarrassed silence.

"I'm sorry about last night," I say after a long moment.

"It's okay. You barely know me, and I was pushing you for personal information. You don't need to tell me anything."

"I was lying awake last night for a long time worrying about it. I figured it wasn't fair to ask you to be friends with me if I don't give anything back."

"You don't have to be friends with me, Dan. No one's forcing you. Alan hoped you would want to be part of the group. The whole concept of Kabballah is about finding Hashem, and the best way to do that is with other people. He will act as a guide and support, but we're more successful together than alone. Don't shut us out."

I take a sip of tea and try to process what she's saying. My tired brain fails.

"You just said I don't have to open up?"

"You don't have to open up to me. But find someone in the group who you can talk to."

"I can't talk to any of the others. After you'd gone last night, they were all being really snide. It was a relief when most of them left, but Simon and Anthony stayed over." They had each bagged a spare bedroom, leaving me with the sofa. "Alan was kind and got me stuff to sleep in, and the sleeping bag, but I didn't exactly feel welcome."

"Last night I thought you were going to talk to me, while we were outside I mean." Rachel looks puzzled, and another nugget of guilt gnaws at my stomach, adding to all the other nuggets that have been there all night.

"I know. Anger got me that far. By the time we'd finished washing up, I lost the impetus to carry on talking. I'm sorry." I glance at her. She looks puzzled and a bit hurt. Shit. "I suppose you want to know what happened with Rick?"

"Who's Rick?"

"My friend. The one I mentioned last night."

"The one who passed away?"

"Yeah. The police don't know if he did it himself, or if someone killed him." I try not to think about what I'm saying, but bile rises to my throat anyway.

Rachel reaches over and rests a hand on my shoulder. "That's awful. I'm so sorry. And I had no right to push you for that information. I can't begin to guess how you feel right now."

"Me neither, to tell the truth. I'm still numb." It was only four days ago. How the hell am I supposed to work out how I feel? "If I'm being completely honest, I'll admit that I'm scared to experience any emotion. Every time I've got close, it crushes me." I stand up. I don't think I can even talk about this any more. "Look, I hope Alan won't be offended, or you either, but I think I need to get back this morning. I forgot to tell my friend Becky that I was going to be away, and she'll freak out if she can't find me."

"How will you get back?"

"I've got some cash on me. I know it's against the rules of Shabbat to carry money, and certainly to spend it, but I'm not religious, and never have been. If you can point me to the nearest bus stop into town, I'll get the bus, then another one back to Halls."

"Sure, Dan. I'll show you the way. You should let Alan know though."

"I'll write him a note. I want to thank him anyway."

"Thank who?" Alan's voice from the doorway startles me.

"Hi Alan. I'm really sorry, but I have to get back. I've probably spoilt Shabbat for you."

"No, it's fine. Perhaps it was too soon for you. How's your head?"

"A bit sore still." It isn't really, but it feels like a better excuse than saying I hate all but one of his friends.

"Fine. Hopefully you'll come back in a couple of weeks when things have eased off a bit."

Crikey. Do I have to? I try not to let my horror show on my face, but probably fail.

"Seriously. Come back in a fortnight, or three weeks if you prefer. And get the bus. I know you and Simon didn't quite gel. We have different people each time, but phone me and I'll make sure Rache is here, so you'll at least have one friendly face other than mine."

"Okay, thanks." I feel obliged to accept, however much I don't want to.

"And look, stay in touch. I need to know you're okay. I know you've not had a great time, but you're part of the family now."

Twenty minutes later, I'm on the bus back into Manchester. Rachel walked me to the bus stop as promised, and thankfully it had stopped raining for the walk. I thanked her and gave her a brief hug to say goodbye. She seemed sad, and guilt assails me again as I wonder if my own anxiety has come at the expense of her well-being. We don't know each other that well though. I failed to open up except on the key fact in my life. Nothing else seems to matter, but perhaps I didn't manage to convey that properly.

I'm going to have to go back. I don't want to, but I feel as though I've left unfinished business.

The journey to Halls takes over an hour. Far too long to think, and I battle against the thoughts that keep surfacing. Rick creeps into my head as soon as I relax my guard. I stare out of the window of the bus from town to Fallowfield, but see nothing of the world outside. Rick's face stares reproachfully back at me. I can see him as clearly as if he were right in front of me.

"*Why did you leave me alone that night?*" he seems to say. "*If you'd stayed, I'd have still been alive.*"

I shut my eyes tight, but I can still see his face. Still hear his voice. Still feel the guilt that's been eating away at me since Tuesday. I clench my fists, digging my nails into my palms as hard as I can, forcing the pain, even though my nails are too short to draw blood.

Why did I leave him that night? We'd argued. A stupid row triggered by a sometime girlfriend of his. He'd told me about her, almost bragging about the sexy letters they exchanged. He showed me one, before putting it carefully back in his suitcase out of sight. The care with which he handled the letter inflamed me. Jealousy clawed at me, and I stood right in front of him, suddenly unsure what to do. I don't remember starting it, but somehow next minute we were kissing passionately. It lasted just a moment or two, then he pushed me away and I fell back against the door.

His words will stay with me forever: "*I can't be friends with a gay.*"

His tone stung. It was full of contempt. "What if you've got AIDS? What if you've just given it to me? I've enough problems without that. Why the fuck did you have to kiss me? Why couldn't we have just stayed friends?"

That was the point at which I left his room. Next morning, he was dead.

I clamp my hand over my mouth and run to the front of the bus. The driver glances at me, and stops the bus. I jump off and throw up at the side of the road, vomiting until there's nothing left. I sit weakly on the ground, with my back against a wall. As soon as a bit of energy returns, I look around. I'm only a few minutes' walk from Halls. I drag myself to my feet, and stumble my way, almost falling into the Tower building when I arrive. I wait for the lifts. Numbness has returned. I can no longer think about that night, but I'm vaguely aware that I'm missing something. A hidden meaning in the words he spoke that night that eludes me – perhaps because I'm not ready to face it.

In the foyer of the tenth floor, I glance at my watch. Nine-thirty. Is it too early to knock on Becky's door? Probably, but in case she's been up all night panicking about me, I'd better check. I turn right, away from the lifts and towards her room. I only tap gently, but there's an instant response.

"Who is it?" I barely recognise the voice. She sounds shaky and distressed.

"Becks? It's me, Dan. Are you okay?"

The door opens, and Becky stands there in her pyjamas. Her face is pale and tear-stained, there's a cut on her cheek, and her hair is a wreck.

"Come in," she says. Shutting the door behind me, she throws herself at me and bursts into tears.

Chapter Fifteen
Saturday 28/1/89

Becky

I let Dan hold me for several minutes, savouring the rare pleasure of an extended hug. But tears of relief dry quickly, and I can't fake it. Eventually, I sniff and pull back.

"Thank you. I needed that."

"Me too. But what on earth happened? I've never seen you this upset." Dan sits down on the bed with his legs stretched out in front of him. I take advantage of the moment, and sit next to him. He puts his arm around me, and I rest my head on his shoulder.

"I got attacked."

"What? How? Are you okay?"

"It's usually me that asks all the questions, and I'm saving a few for later."

"Becky…!" There's a warning note in his voice, and I can tell he's waiting for me to answer him.

"Okay. I ran out of cash. I'd left my card on my desk. I'd had the day from hell at Uni, and was walking home wondering how not to get thrown off my course, when these lads grabbed me and pulled me away from the main road."

Dan pulls his arm away and turns sideways to look at me. "What happened to your cheek?" He sounds concerned, but a bit calmer than before I started talking.

"One of them had a knife. He held it my cheek. I guess it nicked the skin when I pressed my rape alarm – they all seemed a bit stunned, so I took advantage and ran." I glance down at the still-messy floor – assorted clothes and books, spattered with a few drops of blood. "They made some awful threats before I pressed the alarm."

"You got away. That's what matters. Have you told the police?"

"Yes." I hesitate. Do I tell him about clearing out Rick's room? I don't want to keep secrets from Dan, but this would upset him. I decide to keep it simple. "While you were out, I met a lady Sergeant – Wendy. She gave me her number so I called her when I got back yesterday. She's really nice." Not exactly the whole truth, but it'll suffice for now.

"Good. I hope they catch the bastards. Are you okay though? You still seem shaky."

"I am. It freaked me out. But I don't really want to talk about it any more. What have you been up to? Were you out all night?" I try to keep any hint of accusation from my voice, but in between nightmares about the attack, I'd lain awake half the night wondering where Dan was.

"Long story."

"So tell me. There's no rush – I've only got the essay from hell to worry about, and frankly it can wait."

I listen while Dan tells me all about his trip to this Kabbalistic group.

"Will you go back?" I ask when he stops talking.

"I dunno. Rachel was nice to me, and Alan was okay too. I guess if they're going to be there, and some of the others are absent, it might be alright."

"What did you think of the religious…" I stop myself from saying 'claptrap' just in time; "…er… side of things?"

"It pissed me off last night, but I was thinking about it on the bus home. It sort of made sense. They're trying to get closer to God, and some of what they were doing was just hypocritical bullshit, but some of it felt genuine. There was one guy – I'd kind of almost forgotten about him, but he popped into my head on the bus – he'd been depressed. He didn't say why. But he'd spent a few minutes at the end of each day praying, and thanking God for the good things that had happened. He said the first few days had been almost impossible, and he stayed away last week because he felt like a failure, but then he kept trying, and little things would come back to him each night that made him feel a bit better. Anyway, I'm going to give it a try." He looks at the floor for a minute, and flushes, before looking me in the eye. "If nothing else, I can thank God for giving me you as a friend."

Words desert me, and tears fill my eyes. I grab his hand and squeeze it hard while I try to pull myself together.

"Bloody hell, Dan. That's mutual, but thank you. I reckon that's the nicest thing anyone has ever said to me." We hug again. I know it's only platonic, but I can copy Dan and thank God that at least I have him as a friend. When we pull away, I'm not the only one with wet cheeks, and I reckon it's time to change the subject.

"I have to rewrite the essay from hell. Have you got any work to do?"

"I've done sweet F.A. since Tuesday. I think I might have an assignment or something to be in next week. I ought to have a look."

"Do you fancy checking, and then coming to the library with me? We can slog through together." I vaguely recall Greg mentioning something about the library, but I'd rather go with Dan. I don't know Greg properly, and, well, he can't compete.

Seven hours later and we're on the bus back from the John Rylands library – my essay and Dan's assignment complete – exhausted but relieved.

"Thanks for coming with me, Dan. I wouldn't have got it finished without you. Hopefully it'll pass this time."

"No problem. I'd never have got mine done either. I'd kind of forgotten about it, to be honest. Do you fancy a pizza?"

My stomach growls at the thought.

"Guess that's a yes then!" Dan grins. It's the first time I've seen him smile since before Tuesday, and whilst I'm embarrassed at the loudness of my abdominal organs, it's a relief to see him relax.

The relaxed, teasing state lasts until we're in the takeaway.

"Hey, Daniel. Where's your mate, Rick? He owes me

twenty quid." The speaker is a short, pallid-looking guy of about our age. I don't recognise him, but take an instant dislike to him. I don't wait for Dan to respond.

"Rick's dead, and so's your money. Sod off and leave us alone." Fortunately our pizza boxes arrive on the counter at this point, and I hand over a ten-pound note in payment. I grab the boxes as the stranger lunges for them.

"I reckon they're mine – at least I'll take them in lieu of my twenty quid." He reaches out to claim our dinner, but Dan rams his knuckles into the guy's chest, then grabs my wrist. We run as the guy doubles over. I glance back and see him clasping his chest. When we're back in the lift, breathless but still in possession of the pizza, I turn to Dan.

"Thanks." I take a lungful of air and breathe out slowly. "What did you do to him?"

"This." He shows me his fist, with his middle knuckle sticking out by half an inch. "Jab this into a certain part of the chest. It makes them think they've been stabbed. I learned it in judo when I was little. I've never forgotten that one, and I've used it a few times over the years. Any time anyone wanted to pick on me. They didn't do it again." The lift arrives on the tenth floor and we get out.

"I need to learn that stuff. It might help if I ever get into a situation like yesterday."

"It's useful." Dan falls quiet for a moment as we head from the lift to my room. Once we're inside he looks at me with a frown. "Why would Rick owe money to a stranger, and how did he know my name?"

Chapter Sixteen
Saturday 4/2/89

Daniel

I lie on my bed brooding about the last week. The only thing that's got me through has been Becky's friendship.

There were a few minutes last Saturday when I was able to forget, just very briefly, about the agony that I was in. Then that git in the pizza place spoilt it. I've not been able to regain those moments, but I've spent a lot of time wondering who he was, and why Rick would have owed him money. I'm still none the wiser.

With my head wound healing, the dressing off and my hair beginning to regrow, I returned to lectures on Tuesday; exactly one week from THAT DAY. Well, I reckon if we'd still been friends, and Rick had been alive, he'd have told me to go back to Uni. It helps… a bit. I can't concentrate, but for a few minutes at a time, I listen to the lecturers and pretend that everything is normal, and that my heart's not shattered. Such a cliché really, but it feels like a cleaving in my chest, so perhaps it's reasonably accurate.

My ability to cope with the pain varies from one minute to the next. Becky's presence always helps. Having her there stops me feeling quite so alone, even though I don't love her the same way I loved Rick, or the way she loves me. Yes, she does – I'd be stupid not to have noticed. She tries to hide it, and maybe I'm horrible to let it carry on, but I reckon she's sussed me out by now, and if she couldn't handle being friends, she'd let me know. So I bury any guilt I might feel about stringing her along, and keep going to her for comfort, sympathy and chocolate hobnobs. She provides each in abundance, and I think I must be addicted to all three.

Rachel and Alan have taken turns to call me each night. They must be in cahoots, as they never both call on the same night, and there's never an evening when I don't hear from one of them. Their chatter is casual – asking me how I am, and talking about the weather, sport or politics, and the state of the roads, where the potholes seem to get worse every day. I honestly don't give a damn about any of the topics, but it's kind of nice to hear their voices, I guess. My feelings towards them both are confused. Perhaps the belief that they're discussing me behind my back detracts from any feelings of friendship that try to surface. Other than that, I like them. They're friendly and they seem to care about me. Apart from Becky, they're the only ones who do.

I sent my dad and sister a letter on Monday, telling them that a friend had died in suspicious circumstances. That letter took about two hours and twenty discarded sheets of paper before I got a result I was prepared to put in the post. I've not heard a thing from them. I thought at least Cathy would have phoned me. She's two years younger than me, but we were always close growing up. There's another notch of pain when I think she might have abandoned me too. I don't suppose I expected Dad to give me a call. He's always been too busy with his business mergers to give two hoots about his son.

So it's now Saturday again. I declined an invitation from Alan to go back there this week, but said I might go next weekend instead. But now I wish I'd gone. Becky is off for the day doing some self-defence course. It'll be good for her; she's lost confidence since being attacked by those lads. It leaves me alone though.

For lack of anything better to do, I fill up a laundry bag with some washing. It's overdue, and I've not really had any clean clothes to wear for the last few days. I grab a book to keep me occupied while the machine's on, but I don't hold out much hope.

When I arrive in the launderette, there are a few other students seated on the benches. No one pays me any attention; they all seem to be with friends. Why did I come alone? The loneliness ramps up a few notches. I grimace to myself and load up the nearest empty washer. By the time it's loaded with detergent, clothes and money, I feel a bit calmer, and sit on the bench, taking the book out of my rucksack. It's a David Eddings, and I was enjoying it when I could discuss the details with Rick. We'd been at the same point more or less, but I've not been able to look at it since… Anyway, it was a bad idea to bring it today. I seem to have lost interest in the tension between Garion and Ce'nedra, and whether Garion is a sorcerer or not. Okay, if I'm being totally honest, I've not lost interest, but the thought of reading it without discussing it afterwards leaves a huge hole in me. I put the book back in my bag, and watch the machine spinning. It's like my thoughts – all those horrible ideas rushing around in my head, sucking in blood instead of water.

I return again to the events of that night, and the final argument. It seemed like the end of the world at the time. I didn't realise it actually was…

I couldn't sleep afterwards, and knocking on his door the next morning was inevitable. I had to find out if he really meant it, and if our friendship was over. When he didn't answer, I banged on the door loudly, shouting his name. The lack of response annoyed and then scared me, but I remember going to Martin and asking if he could open the door. He had to call Security; I would have thought a house tutor should have had keys. I must have waited about twenty minutes, hammering on the door and calling out.

"Hey, Rick, please just answer the door. Are you okay? Why are you not answering? Please open the sodding door, come on."

The guys on either side of Rick's room came out after a while; Stuart and Nathan were dressed for Uni, but glared at me anyway, and harangued me for the noise. I muttered an apology, but otherwise ignored them. Security had just arrived.

"Why do you need to get into another student's room?" asked the guy – a small thin chap with a moustache. He

didn't look as if he'd be much good in a fight, but I suppose not all security people need to be built like wrestlers. His tone was interrogating, and I responded quickly.

"I'm worried that he's not answering. Normally he'd have let me in before now, or at least shout to come back later. There's no response at all."

The security guard unlocked the door with a huge set of keys that he extracted from a sports-type bag on his shoulder. The door opened...

"Are you alright, mate? You look a bit peaky." A guy in a navy sweatshirt and jogging bottoms taps me on the shoulder, interrupting my horrific recollections.

"Yes, thanks." I manage a weak smile.

What am I doing here? I can't escape the thoughts of what happened that day. The image of Rick slumped on the desk will stay with me for ever. I remember going in and putting my fingers on his cold skin to try and find a pulse. But I knew as soon as I touched him. I see him every time I close my eyes. The only other image that competes with it is that of Rick's face when he told me he couldn't be friends with me any more. The scorn and contempt haunts me, day and night. I feel my insides shrivel. I don't know if I can carry on with this.

I walk outside. The washing will still be a while yet, but I don't care about it just now. It's cold out, and the biting wind matches my mood, howling in despair, as I wish I could howl. The noise is inside my head all the time, trying to escape. But I have to force myself to keep it within me.

As I walk, heaven knows where, the despair fills me, taking over my whole being. I become one with the howling wind, moving independently of thought.

Although perhaps not, as I find myself climbing the steps of a railway footbridge.

Chapter Seventeen
Saturday 4/2/89

Becky

I arrive in a community hall in South Manchester at the specified time – 11am – and look around me. There are half a dozen girls of around my age chatting together in a corner. Most of the floor is covered in the sort of blue matting seen in judo competitions. Butterflies dance in my stomach. They must be practising – warming up for the real action.

A giant of a man emerges from another room.

"Hello, luv, are you here for the self-defence class?"

"Yes." I manage to keep my voice from shaking. I'm ridiculously nervous.

"We're nearly ready to start – just waiting for one more. Take off any jewellery, and also your shoes and socks."

I nod, and sit on the floor not far from the other girls. One of them glances at me and comes over.

"Hi, I'm Theresa. Is this your first time here?" Theresa is about my height, with straight dark hair in a ponytail, and a friendly smile.

"Yes. How about you? Oh, and I'm Becky."

"Hi Becky. This is my second time, but I'm so uncoordinated, I thought I should come back to get the hang of things a bit better. What made you decide to come along?"

"Some lads got hold of me on my way home from Uni. I was lucky to get away. I figured some techniques might come in handy."

She nods, and grimaces. "I guess it's one of the perils of being at Uni in a big city. I come from a village in the Lake District. I wouldn't leave my door open, but it's a pretty safe place." She looks over at the other girls and lowers her voice.

"Everyone I met here last time has some sort of story to tell – an attack or near miss."

"What about you? I don't mean to pry if you don't want to tell me, though."

She looks around again, and waits for me to stand up before whispering in my ear. "I've got a problem with one of my lecturers. He's my tutor, and he's taken to arranging private tutorials. He's bigger than me, and it's hard to push him away. At least this gives me some techniques to help."

"Can't you tell anyone? In authority, I mean?"

"He's really senior. Who would I tell?"

"Okay, girls. Come on, it's time to get started."

"Pair with me," whispers Theresa.

I nod, and go and stand next to her. The next hour we grow quite friendly as we take it in turns to try to break out of various different holds, but there are no opportunities to discuss her situation until we have a break.

With cans of coke in front of us, from a vending machine in the entrance foyer, we finally get a chance to speak in quiet voices a little away from the other girls and the instructors.

"So, I've been thinking about your tutor situation, and I reckon you should speak to one of the advisors in the Students' Union."

"Thanks, Becky. That's not a bad idea. I suppose they're here to help us, not to immediately grass us out to the lecturers."

"Absolutely. In fact, I'm thinking about going to them myself. Not for quite the same reason, but my tutor is a real bully, and he's threatening to have me thrown off the course. My work is no worse than anyone else's, but he's horrible."

"I think I'd rather have that though. At least you're not physically threatened."

"No, that's true. Just my career." Seeing her frown, I laugh. I don't want to antagonise her – we've only just met. "I'm joking. An abuser is far worse than a bully. You must speak to someone about it and get it sorted. That sort thrive on silence. Both types really."

She relaxes a bit, and turns the conversation to the techniques we've just practised.

The second half of the session is even more fun, with some interactions with the instructors. One of them, a tall thin guy named Jez, starts the segment by saying, "We don't want you to hurt each other, so you'll practise the next few moves on us."

By the time ten girls have inflicted pain on the three instructors in several different ways, I realise I've had a lot of fun. Theresa seems to have forgotten our brief altercation, and I've exchanged smiles and laughs with the other girls in the group too. I'm not sure I'm ready to do any of the techniques for real, but the sessions are held every other week, so I'm determined to come back and learn more.

Outside, after the class is finished, Theresa and I exchange phone numbers and addresses. She lives in the same Halls as me, but in a different block. We agree to meet up on Wednesday afternoon to go to see the student advisor in the Union.

"Are you going back to Halls now?" I ask.

"No, I'm off into town. I need to get my mum a birthday present. Do you want to come with?"

An image appears in my head of Dan alone in his room, and I shake my head. "Sorry, but I need to get back. One of my friends is having a bad time. I need to check he's okay."

"No problem. See you Wednesday."

I wave goodbye, and head to the bus stop. It's broad daylight, but I'm still very twitchy about walking anywhere. Fifteen minutes later, I knock on Dan's door. There's no reply.

"Dan, are you there?" I call out.

Sanjay comes out of his room. "I saw him earlier heading out with a bundle of clothes. I think he might have been going to the launderette."

"Thanks, Sanj. I don't know why, but I've got a weird feeling in my gut. I think I need to check up on him."

"Good luck with that, Becks." He laughs, then gives me a second glance. "Okay. Do you want company?"

"If you've got time, yes please."
"Okay, I'll grab my coat. Give me a minute."

The launderette is full, with a lot of students sitting around watching machines go round and round. On the floor, in front of one of the machines, is a pile of clothes that on closer inspection I recognise as possibly Dan's.

"Excuse me?" I tap the shoulder of the girl watching the machine near the clothes pile. "Do you know whose these are? Who took them out of the machine?"

"I've no idea whose they are, but someone said this guy had been here, and just wandered off, leaving all his stuff in the machine. All the other washers are full, so I had to take his stuff out."

"And dump it on the floor?" I don't bother keeping the sarcasm out of my voice. It's less revealing than the fear that is beginning to take hold of me. There's a black bin liner on the top of one of the machines. I shiver, remembering the last time I had to shove things in a bin liner. No comparison to Rick of course, but I wish I knew where Dan has gone.

When all his clothes are in the bag, I look at Sanjay.

"Any ideas?" My voice sounds hoarse, and Sanjay gives me a concerned look before turning to the other girl.

"Is the guy still here? The one who saw our friend leave?"

"No, but I know him. He lives two door down from here." She gives Sanjay the door number, and we take the bag of clothes with us to knock on the man's door. A tall, tanned guy in his late twenties or early thirties answers, and looks confused to see two students on his doorstep with a full bin bag.

"Hi. Can I help you at all?" He sounds cultured – more Chelsea than Manchester.

"I believe you saw our friend leave the launderette a short while ago without taking his laundry with him." I see his eyes go to the black bag and comprehension dawning on his face. "Please could you tell us when he left and which direction he went?"

"Yes of course. Do you want to come in a minute? You can

leave your friend's washing with me at least while you go and search for him."

We follow him up some stairs and into a small flat. I look around. It's a little old-fashioned in décor, but is immaculately kept, with everything spotlessly clean and tidy.

"Please sit down for a moment. I'm Tommy, by the way." He looks expectantly at us.

"I'm Becky, and this is Sanjay. Please tell us about our friend. Dan is a little unwell at the moment, and I'm worried about him."

"To be honest, I was a bit concerned too. He was sitting on the bench in the launderette brooding about something. I had to switch my own laundry from the washer to the dryer, and when I turned back, he'd gone, but his washing was still on. I went to the door to look for him, and he was about a hundred yards away, walking towards Withington, but too far to shout to."

"How long ago was that?" Sanjay asks, beating me to it by a second.

Tommy looks at his watch. "About an hour ago, perhaps a bit less. Do you want me to come and help you find him?" He goes to a cupboard, and extracts a large black object that looks a bit like a phone, but with no wires. He puts it into a grey rucksack. "We might need this. It's my mobile phone. We can use it to call the police or an ambulance if your friend is in trouble."

Sanjay and I glance at each other, and I nod briefly. I'm scared, and we might need all the help we can get.

"Thank you." I smile at Tommy. "That's really kind of you to give up your time like this."

"It's fine. Come on. Actually, bring the laundry. We'll go in my car. When we find your friend – Dan, isn't it? – we can deliver you all home with the washing." He grins, and I notice a set of unusually white teeth. I would normally be reluctant to get into a car with a strange man, but I have Sanjay with me, and this might be an emergency. We have to find Dan.

Besides, I'm inclined to like and trust our apparently

wealthy new acquaintance. He must be quite rich to have a device like that. A mobile phone? I have to say it doesn't look brilliantly mobile, but what a great idea.

Tommy leads us to the area at the back of his flat, and to his car: a dark blue Jaguar XJS with leather seats, which reiterates the general impression of wealth, even if he is living in a small flat above a shop in Fallowfield.

The laundry goes into the boot, I get in the back and Sanjay sits in the front, next to the driver. We head in the direction that Dan was last seen.

"Eyes peeled, folks. Obviously you know him better than I do, but when I saw him, he was wearing a blue parka jacket and jeans. Unfortunately, that probably describes half the population of Manchester."

"Do you think there's any chance the police might be able to help us? I have a number for the station at Longsight, and one of the Sergeants there is really helpful." Wendy could help us, and she'd have a lot more resources at her disposal than me, Sanjay and Tommy.

"Sure. Give Sanjay the number. The car phone is better while we're in here than the mobile, so we can dial on that."

"Ask for DS Lucas." I hand Sanjay the card with Wendy's number. "Tell her I gave you the number, and that we're searching for Dan."

"Sure." Sanjay dials, and asks for the DS as instructed. "Oh hi. Yes, my friend Becky gave me the number, but she's in the back of the car. I don't think she can reach the phone from there."

"Hi Wendy," I call out. "Please can you help us?"

I can just about hear her voice replying, "Yes, of course".

Sanjay puts the phone back to his ear and explains the situation. There's silence in the car as he listens to her response. The tension is palpable.

"Where's that?" he asks. "Oh my God." He turns to Tommy. "Do you know the railway bridge near Longsight station?"

Tommy nods, and I can see his expression in the mirror is grim as he takes a swift left then puts his foot on the accelerator.

"Okay. We're heading straight there. Is there anyone with him?"

I try to process what I've heard. When Sanjay replaces the car phone on its holder, he twists his head to look at me. His face is paler than usual and he looks sick.

"He's on the bridge. Talking about jumping. A passer-by saw him climb on to the wall and called the police. There's an officer with him trying to talk him out of it, but even if he changes his mind, there's a chance he could just fall."

I don't respond. I can't speak. Bile fills my throat, and my pulse is shooting through the sunroof. Tommy doesn't look around, but his voice is grave as he says, "We'll be there in about two minutes guys." He must be scanning the roads ahead and to the side, as he edges through a red light, before hitting the accelerator again. Exactly two minutes later we pull up next to a bridge, and I'm out of the car before Tommy's killed the engine.

I look up. Sitting on the bridge, with his legs dangling over the wall facing out to the railway, is Daniel.

Chapter Eighteen
Saturday 4/2/89

Daniel

I don't know how long I've been sitting up here. My mind is blank. I don't even remember climbing over the wall, but here I am, one shuffle away from a quick but very messy death. Do I want to join Rick this way? Would I be able to? If he killed himself, maybe we'd end up in the same place, but unable to see each other. Is suicide a sin in Judaism? I don't even know that.

I glance down. Big mistake. The rails below blur into a fuzzy grey-brown pattern. Nausea rises, but I push it down. How many people get themselves into this position, then change their minds and decided to live after all, only to fall and die anyway? I don't want to be one of them.

Somewhere in the depths of my confused, grief-stricken and agonised being, I know I want to survive this. The awful thing is I haven't a clue how to get back to safety. Sitting on the wall facing the danger is all very well, but the thought of moving just an inch fills me with terror.

A train rumbles underneath me. I feel the vibrations through my body, and tighten my grip on the back edge of the wall.

"Alright lad? What're you doing up there?"

I risk a glance round. A tall policeman with a black moustache matching his helmet and uniform is on the bridge a few feet behind me. He sounds kind.

"I need help." I mean that I need help to get down safely, but he doesn't seem to take it that way.

"I can see you do, lad. Let's get you down from there, and

then we'll see about getting you someone to talk to. This isn't a good way out, believe me."

"How would you know?" I don't mean to sound belligerent, but another train is on its way – I can feel the rumbling of the bridge.

"My brother did this three years ago. He jumped. Bloody wreck he was. I had to identify the body. My mum couldn't face it. Worst sight ever – and I've been in the force fifteen years. Don't do it, lad. It doesn't solve anything."

My teeth start to chatter from the fear and cold, and I'm unable to speak for a few minutes. When I get them under control, all I'm able to say is, "Why?" I risk another glance round at him.

"Why did he jump, you mean?" He rubs his nose and shakes his head slowly. "I don't know for certain. He didn't leave a note. But we found out afterwards that his marriage had broken down. She was having an affair, and threatening to walk out. Bob, my brother, adored that bitch. She didn't even mourn him. Turned up to the funeral in a tarty dress and high heels, and left with this other bloke. If I hadn't been a copper, I'd have beaten him to a pulp, the bastard." He pauses. Another train passes underneath, and my position shifts with the vibration. I'm an inch closer to the edge. Shit. I'm going to die. I really don't want to die.

"Yes – lad on the railway bridge – student, I reckon. Looks ready to jump."

I turn my head a fraction again, but I'm getting too scared to move at all. Out of the corner of my eye, I see him talking into some sort of communicator – a walkie-talkie device.

"What's your name, lad?"

"Daniel."

"I believe there are some friends of yours looking for you. There are people out there who care for you, Daniel. Do not jump. Let's just wait for your friends, and maybe they can talk to you?"

Sod talking. I just want to get down from here. Safely. Maybe if Becky's on her way she can instigate a rescue plan, but for now, I need to stay put until this stupid copper realises

I'm shitting myself in case I fall. The thought of jumping, even to possibly meet Rick, has receded a long way.

"Daniel? Do you promise not to jump before your friends arrive? You'll let them talk to you?"

"I promise." I can't promise I won't fall though. My fingers are numb from cold and from gripping the back edge of the wall so tightly. I can barely feel them any more, but I don't know how else to grip. Minutes pass in silence. I guess the policeman is just happy that I've promised to wait for whoever's coming for me. God, please let it be Becky.

In the distance, a car door slams – at least, that's what it sounds like. I risk a glance down and to the side, anxious to see who's coming to help. There's a moment before anyone comes into sight, then Becky, Sanjay and a stranger appear on the road next to the railway tracks.

"Dan! You stay where you are. We're coming to help you. Do not move!" Becky shouts up. She sounds hoarse, and guilt shoots through me for upsetting her. Then another train rumbles beneath me, and fear takes over. What if I can't hang on? My hands are clammy now, and grip seems to be diminishing. Only the balance of my bottom on the wall is keeping me steady, and that's so precarious, it could go any moment.

"Okay, Dan. I'm behind you. Don't panic. I'm going to grab hold of you, and then Sanjay and Tommy are going to help me bring you to safety. We'll talk to you properly when you're on solid ground." Her arms go around my waist, and then I feel strong grips on either arm. I'm hauled backwards over the wall, and collapse weakly to the pavement.

Chapter Nineteen
Saturday 4/2/89

Becky

It's been three hours since Dan's rescue on the bridge, and I'm now sitting on the chair in his room. He's curled up on his bed fully dressed in jeans and sweatshirt, ignoring the pizza and hobnobs on the desk. I get up and turn on the cassette player on the window ledge, but get a dirty look for my pains.

"What's wrong?" I ask, as *Ship of Fools* by Erasure emerges from the speakers.

"Can't listen to that. No Erasure, no Abba. Find something else."

I raise my eyebrows at his abrupt tone, but skim through the titles of cassette tapes on the storage unit at the end of his bed. There's a ridiculous number of cassettes by the two banned artists, and a large quantity of home-made compilations in Rick's handwriting. I don't even bother suggesting those. Finally, "How about Depeche Mode?"

"Okay, that'll do. Yeah. That's fine." He sits up, but slowly, as if reluctant. "What happened to my laundry?"

"Tommy took it. He said he'd get it re-washed and dried for you, after some miserable cow pulled it onto the floor. He'll drop it in tomorrow." I put the tape in the machine and press *Play*.

"Oh yeah. I forgot he said that. Thanks." He hugs his knees. "I don't think I've thanked you properly for saving my life."

"You can thank me by not doing it again." I sit down and take a hobnob from the packet, but my appetite evaporates as the physical memory of seeing Dan on the bridge takes hold of my body. I force myself to take a bite, but the biscuit is like sawdust in my mouth. "What made you do it, Dan? I got the impression that by the time I got there, you'd given up all idea of jumping."

"God, yeah. I was just petrified I was going to fall. I honestly don't know how I got there. One minute I was brooding about... well, you know... in the launderette, then I kind of went into a weird trance. I woke up – if you can call it that – and I was on that sodding bridge. That bloody copper thought I wanted to jump. He never bothered to ask, let alone to hang on to me, to stop me from falling."

"Maybe he was frightened that if you did jump, you'd take him over with you." I put the remains of the hobnob on the desk.

"Perhaps. Either way. I can't tell you how relieved I was to see you."

"Same here. I was terrified we'd be too late."

"Hey, come here." Dan reaches out his arms, and I go and sit facing him on the bed, leaning into him for a huge hug that lasts for a long time. I think it's a release of tension for both of us, because I can feel his sobs vibrate against me, as I'm sure mine do against him. When the hug ends, both our faces are wet with tears. "I won't do it again, I promise."

He'd better be meaning the bridge, rather than the hug, but I'm too emotionally drained to quibble about it.

"Do you need to talk to someone? Professionally I mean?" I ease over to perch on the edge of the bed.

"Other than the bloody police doctor they had me closeted with for over an hour?" He gives me a dark look, and I retreat back to the chair. He takes a deep breath. "I think maybe I should try Alan again. See if this Kabbalah thing helps."

"Do you want me to call him?"

"Later probably." He glances out of the window, and I follow his gaze. "It's still Shabbat. Not sure what time it goes out, but we'd better wait until it's dark."

"Sure." I'm not religious at all. We never kept Shabbat at home, but I've been to enough youth weekends to have an idea of the basics. "I'll call him after dinner."

Dan manages to raise a smile, although it's a bit feeble. "Isn't that dinner?" He nods towards the unopened pizza box.

I shrug, and am about to say something non-committal, when there's a knock at the door. I raise my eyebrows at Dan, and he nods.

I open the door to Sanjay.

"Dan, mate, are you okay? You gave us a hell of a fright."

"Sorry. I didn't mean to. If it makes you feel any better, I scared myself too."

"Good. That means you won't do it again. Have you thawed out yet?"

"Just about. Do you want pizza? Neither Becky nor I seem to be hungry."

Sanjay comes in and takes a large slice. He shoves a load in his mouth, and perches on the desk.

"Cheers," he mumbles with his mouth full. I catch Dan's eye, and stifle a laugh. He looks horrified. He's told me on so many occasions that he can't stand bad manners, and he includes such breaches of etiquette as stuffing one's face before speaking. It lightens the mood though. The room is still filled with tension, despite the company, the music and the food.

Sanjay at least waits until he's finished his mouthful before opening his mouth again.

"We've all been asked to attend a suicide awareness thing on Monday evening. I reckon it's because of you and Rick." Sanjay nods at Dan, who blanches. Sanjay doesn't appear to notice, as he carries on talking. "They were shoving leaflets under doors just now. I don't know why you've not got one."

"Maybe whoever was delivering them had the sensitivity not to deliver one here. Not that Dan shouldn't discuss this, but I think it would be better done in private." I glance over at him, and get a grateful half-smile in return.

"As I was saying to Becks, it wasn't my intention to jump. I kind of got there by accident."

Sanjay raises his eyebrows, and I jump in to change the subject, dragging it as far away from personal issues as possible by asking Sanjay if he's seen the latest episode of *EastEnders*. I notice Dan retreat into a daze, but at least the attention is away from him.

"I'd better go," says Sanjay after a few minutes. "Any chance of another slice of pizza?"

Dan rouses himself to answer. "Sure. Thanks for popping in."

When the door closes behind his neighbour, he looks at me. "He's a nice guy, but…"

"Sensitivity of a tea-towel?"

"Yeah, something like that."

There's a moment's silence. I get up and look out of the window. It's dark now and raining, and relief floods through me that we're safe inside.

"You do believe that I didn't mean to do it, don't you?" asks Dan. His face is paler than it was when Sanjay left, and his voice shakes slightly.

"Of course I do. But there was a bit of you – maybe only a small bit – that got you there in the first place. I want to make sure that it doesn't talk louder next time. Do you think it's time to call Alan?"

He glances at the window.

"Yeah, probably. Are you sure you don't mind calling? I've got a pile of 10p pieces in that drawer." He points to the top drawer of his desk, and I open it. Unlike mine, it's scrupulously clean and tidy; the money is sitting in a holder separating out different coin types. I grab a few 10p coins, and wait while Dan writes the number down for me, before going to the payphone in the foyer.

Amy from my corridor is on the phone, looking settled as if planning to chat for an hour. I catch her attention, and mouth "How long?"

"Mum, I'm going to have to go – someone needs the phone urgently." She waits for a moment. "I don't know why, but she's a friend. She wouldn't throw me off for nothing." A minute later, she puts the phone down.

"Thanks, and sorry for cutting your call short."

"Short? Mum's been wittering at me for the last hour. I

was kind of glad for the excuse. How's Dan? Sanj said he'd been in a bit of trouble." She looks genuinely concerned, and I remember she's on the same course as Dan.

"Yes, he has really. I need to call a friend of his – an adult, a proper adult – who might be able to help."

"Sure, go ahead. I'll leave you in peace. Say hi to Dan from me. Tell him I wish him well."

"Thanks Amy, I will do." I flash her a smile, and she turns and leaves the foyer. I wait until the door closes before picking up the phone.

I dial the number and wait for an answer. My heart's thumping. How do I tell a religious leader that someone he was beginning to mentor nearly killed himself?

The phone rings out for ages, and I'm about to give up, when there's a click. I insert money quickly.

"Hello, Alan speaking. Who is it?"

"Oh hi. Er, this is Becky, Dan's friend."

"Dan? Oh yes, Daniel – the student. Yes of course. Is everything okay, Becky?"

"Kind of. Dan's safe in his room, so that's good, but he had a bit of a funny turn today, and ended up on a bridge. He says now that he didn't want to jump, but that he was in a trance. By the time he woke up from it, he was in a really dangerous position." I don't go in to detail about how he actually got down. Time's short. I put another coin in the slot. This blasted phone eats money like a hungry giant.

There's a brief silence on the other end of the line. I assume Alan is processing what I've just told him. I need to hurry him up a bit.

"Can you come and visit him please, Alan?"

"Yes, of course. I can pop down tomorrow if that works." His voice sounds overly polite – maybe a little hesitant, but I put it down to shock at what's happened.

"Great, thanks. What sort of time?"

"I'll be there at eleven. I'll bring bagels. Maybe you'd like to join us at midday? Then I can have an hour with Dan before lunch. What do you think?"

"That sounds lovely, thanks." I say goodbye and ring off,

just beating the pips.

I return to Dan's room to tell him to prepare for his visitor in the morning.

Chapter Twenty
Sunday 5/2/89

Daniel

It takes me ages to get to sleep. I'm seriously freaked out by what's happened today, but I've got Alan coming round in the morning, and I need to sound sane and sensible when he arrives. Eventually I drop off at about three, and wake again four hours later, feeling foggy-headed and gritty-eyed.

I force myself to get up and shower and dress, then knock on for Becky at just gone eight. Miraculously, she's awake. She opens her door to allow me an uninterrupted view of pink check pyjamas and un-brushed hair.

"Dan, you're up. Are you okay?"

"I guess so. I reckon I should have some breakfast. Maybe a slice of toast. Do you want to join me? Perhaps get dressed first?"

She promises to pick me up from my room in about ten minutes. From long experience, I know she means twenty, but that's fine. I return to my room, and start to tidy it. It's not in too bad a state, but there are a few crumbs around from last night's pizza. There's a vacuum cleaner in the cupboard next to the bathrooms, and I grab it to give my room a quick blitz before breakfast. I'm just putting the vac away when Becks appears, in more normal attire of jeans, sweatshirt and trainers. Her hair has been tamed, for the moment at least.

We're sitting in the dining room with toast and coffee before she says anything beyond trivialities.

"What are you going to say to Alan?"

"I don't know yet. Tell him what happened, I suppose."

"Does he know about Rick?"

"What about Rick?" I ask cautiously. Even now, I don't know how much Becky knows. I suspect not much.

"What is there to tell?" she counters, then looks apologetic. "Sorry, Dan, forget I said that. I just meant… Oh, I don't know… I suppose Alan just needs to know that Rick died in tragic circumstances. Isn't that the standard terminology?" Her tone is bitter, and despite the horrible gnawing in my gut that returned as soon as Rick's name was mentioned, a spark of curiosity forces me to speak.

"What does it matter to you?"

"What do you mean? Of course it matters to me. He was one of our crowd. He was your closest friend. He was a nice guy. Why would it not matter?"

"You're very sweet, thank you. I suppose it's easy to assume that because it affected me so much, that no one else really cared. I've been very selfish as usual."

"You're not selfish. It's really hard to know what to say sometimes, so I guess we just try to carry on as normal. Then you're left thinking no one is bothered. We should all talk more." She looks directly at me with a sympathetic smile. "I am bothered. I know it can't be to the same extent as you, but I can imagine how I'd feel if something like that happened to one of my best friends." She looks away for a moment, and stares out of the window as she says, "That came home to me only too clearly yesterday."

Shit. She's right. I threatened to deprive her of my company. I don't want to make out like I'm the same to her as Rick was to me, but maybe there's less difference than I thought.

"I'm sorry." I don't know what else to say, so scramble around my head for a safe topic of conversation. "Hey, weren't you at that self-defence class yesterday? How did it go?"

The next twenty minutes passes amicably enough while she tells me about her class. I listen with half an ear. The rest of me is wondering what on earth I'm going to discuss with Alan for an hour.

I'm back in my room ten minutes before he's due to arrive. I made Becky rush in the end, because I was scared we'd be late, so now I'm pacing my room, stopping to rearrange things on my desk and shelves every time I pass. After a few minutes, I check my watch. Still five minutes to go. I sit down and bite my nails. Last time I saw him was when I walked out of his house after the Sabbath from hell. He was nice on the phone last time I spoke to him, but I'm panicking that I've offended him. Maybe he won't turn up? I stand up again, and resume pacing. At two minutes past the time he was due, there's a knock on the door. My heart starts pounding, and I find myself sweating. I open the door, and he's standing there smiling and holding a carrier bag, which is emitting the friendly and familiar smell of kosher deli bagels.

"Hi Dan, how are you doing?"

"Fine thanks. Come in." I stand aside and direct him towards the comfy chair at the side of the desk. I sit on the less welcoming desk chair.

He puts the bag on the floor next to him and leans back in the chair.

"Your friend said you had a bit of a funny turn. What happened?"

"She's right. I kind of lost track of what I was doing, and ended up on a bridge over the railway, with my legs facing the scary way. By the time I knew where I was, it was too late to turn around. Becky rescued me."

"That's one hell of a funny turn. What were you thinking about before you lost track of what you were doing?" He gives me a sideways glance.

I can't work out whether he's genuinely sympathetic, or just quizzing me for some reason of his own. I hesitate, unsure how much to say.

"I can't help you if you don't talk to me, you know. Come on. You remember what we said about Kabballah. It's about finding Hashem. You'll only find him if you do things that will make you happier and more fulfilled. Getting rid of demons by talking about them is a big step towards that." He unsuccessfully tries to stifle a yawn. "Sorry, I had a late night last night. Rachel came round, and… well, you know."

I smile and nod. I'm a bit surprised though. I knew he fancied her and that maybe it was reciprocated. Perhaps I thought she was religious enough to want to save herself for marriage. Clearly I was mistaken.

"Anyway, you were about to tell me your thoughts that you were having before you went all peculiar and climbed on to the bridge."

Damn – I thought he'd been distracted.

"I was thinking about Rick, my friend that died. I'm always thinking about him. I try not to. I really do try. I force myself to focus on what other people are saying. I listen to music. I read. I even study. Everything leads back to him. And I can't handle it."

A gleam of light appears briefly in Alan's eyes. I've no idea what it means, if anything. A second later his face is thoughtful and serious.

"I'm sure we can help you. You do need to allow yourself to grieve, though."

"I might be able to if I knew what had happened to him." I hesitate. Do I know Alan well enough to say this?

"Carry on. You looked as though you were going to say something else." He reaches over and touches me briefly on the shoulder. "You need to start trusting me. I can't help if you don't talk to me."

He's right. I need to open up. He's a religious leader. Surely that's a good place to start.

"Rick and I had an argument. I assume you know I'm gay?" I see Alan nod, so I carry on. "Well, that Monday night I told Rick. I'd thought he knew, but I admitted that I fancied him." I leave out the details about the kiss. I can't admit that to anyone.

"How did he react?"

"He went ballistic and threw me out of his room."

"Ouch." Alan raises his eyebrows.

"Not literally. Anyway, I went back the next morning. By the time I'd got Security to let me in, he was dead." My throat clogs up and tears sting my eyes. I blink, trying to hold them back.

"You can cry if you want. It's not a sign of weakness. I cried when my twin died. I still do sometimes when I think about him."

"How did he die?" I ask, more from politeness than because I care.

"Suicide." Alan's grim expression fills me with a sudden inexplicable fear. "He was driven to it." He shakes his head. "Anyway I'll tell you more about that another time. For now, why don't you tell me how you met Rick?"

This is relatively easy, and I chatter more than normal, telling him about the first couple of weeks in Halls, and shared interests in books, movies and music. Then, finally, there's a knock at the door. I glance at my watch. It's midday.

"That'll be Becky." I get up and open the door. "Come in, Becks."

"Thanks for your phone call, Becky," says Alan, holding out his hand to her. "It's great to know that someone is looking out for Dan."

The gaze she gives him is steady but curious.

"Thanks for coming out to see him. Are you sure it's convenient for me to be here? I can go away if you're deep in discussion?"

Alan and I speak at the same time.

"Please stay," I say, contradicting Alan's comment of "Perhaps that would be better."

The polite façade drops a little from both Becky and Alan, and I begin to realise that they don't seem to like each other much.

"Are those bagels in that bag, Alan?" I know damn well there are bagels, but hopefully the question will trigger Alan's generosity. My appetite has fluctuated between slim and none, but suddenly I'm really hungry. It seems a long time since breakfast, even if it was less than two hours, but then I didn't eat much.

"Yes, of course. I promised bagels and I always keep my promises. Have you got any cutlery or plates, Dan? I've got smoked salmon and cream cheese too." Alan's back to his normal self; any antagonism is hidden, or has disappeared in the face of food.

It's mid-afternoon. Alan's gone and I'm sitting in Becky's room – partly to avoid thinking about Rick, and partly because I came to apologise.

"It's not for you to apologise, Dan. I can see Alan doesn't like me. At least he does me the courtesy of acknowledging I'm the only one on hand to keep an eye on you."

"I know, and thanks. I still feel guilty though, and kind of stuck in the middle. I like both of you. I know I've only met him a few times, but even in that short time, I can see he gets a bit weird occasionally, and goes off into moody silences. But he admitted today that his twin brother committed suicide, so maybe that's why."

Becky's silent for a moment, staring out of the window at the incessant rain. When she turns back to me, she's frowning.

"I'm just saying if you go back there, keep in touch, and let me know how long you're going to be. He told me to look out for you, and that's what I'm doing. I can only do that if I know where you are."

A niggle of doubt creeps into my head, but it's accompanied by guilt. After Becky returned to her room, Alan invited me back for next weekend, but asked me to keep the address secret. I'd thought it a bit of a strange request, but he said he'd been plagued by those who disagreed with his ethos. Torn between them, I compromise.

"If you need them, his contact details are in my address book, in my desk drawer. It'll be fine though. I'm going for next weekend. I'm hoping it'll be better than last time, but I've got to try this Kaballah thing properly. I can't risk a repeat of yesterday."

Chapter Twenty-One
Monday 6/2/89

Becky

I arrive at Uni late for one of Dr Leeson's lectures. Trying to sneak in at the back fails, and he interrupts his discourse to call me out.

"Nice of you to bother, Miss White. Wait behind after the class."

I wouldn't mind so much, but he completely ignores the five students who walk in after me. I spend the rest of the lecture in dread of what's to come.

He'd eventually passed the assignment that I'd had to repeat that awful day, but only because he wasn't in on the Monday, so I'd handed it to the head of department with a full explanation of what had happened, including the attack in the alley. She'd been ever so nice and I reckon she made sure he passed me.

We're due to be given another assignment next week, and I'm dreading that too. Leeson drones on about another aspect of law that bores me rigid. I wish there was a course specialising in Criminal Law, but even if there was, my dad wouldn't have let me do anything so 'unsuitable'. In his view, girls should become lawyers only to deal with divorce, housing or family law. That's what his firm deals with, and he's determined that Ian and I both join him when we're fully qualified. One day I'll stand up to him, but for now, I need to concentrate. I force myself to absorb some of the tutor's words and take notes, as he's likely to question me afterwards.

He finally closes the lecture, adding, "Miss White, don't

forget to remain behind." Pretty damn embarrassing in front of 150 other students.

I shove my notes in my bag and drag myself to the front of the lecture theatre.

"Don't slouch, Miss White. Follow me to my office. We'll talk there." He turns immediately and leaves, striding arrogantly down the corridor. I have to almost run to keep up with him, but remain a couple of paces behind. His office is at the other end of the building, in a small cul-de-sac off the main corridor. It feels a long way from the bulk of students, and other populated areas. I notice the other five doors on the cul-de-sac are all nameless, so probably empty. My heart rate picks up a few more notches.

He holds the door open for me; a surprising gesture until I'm inside, when he shuts the door firmly, and turns the key below the handle. He leans against the door. I stand opposite him, against a bookshelf, but as far away as the small office will allow. The desk is on the right by the window. He shows no desire to sit himself behind it.

"So, Rebecca, I've got you alone finally. I owe you a punishment or two. You went behind my back to get your assignment marked, when I had the misfortune to be laid low with gastric flu. And today, you were late to my lecture."

"S-s-so were several other people. I wasn't the last to arrive."

"You dare to answer me back?" He advances towards me, and for a second I think he's going to strangle me, but no. Next second I'm being brutally kissed, and his right hand is mauling my breast. His left is at the button of my jeans, and fear paralyses me for a moment. Then memories of Saturday's class return to my brain, and I force my knee up to his groin. He recoils with a stifled yell.

"You bitch! What the hell do you think you're doing? Do you want to become a lawyer? You're going the wrong way about it." He's bent double clutching at the sensitive area, now clearly in agony. "If you… tell anyone about this…, you're finished… at this university."

I grab the key he's left on the desk, unlock the door, and

run down the corridor without bothering to reply. I'm out of breath and shaking by the time I get to the main lecture theatre, but pause outside.

Do I really want to go in? I'm late; I've got palpitations, and now that I have time to check, realise that my shirt is askew and my jeans button is undone. I divert to the loos, and tidy myself up a bit, but it's not enough to steady my pulse or prevent me throwing up in one of the cubicles. I slump down on the floor next to the toilet and rest my head on my forearm against the toilet seat.

How did this happen? One minute Leeson was bawling at me for being late, the next minute he's molesting me. Seriously? Why would he do that? Am I supposed to let him do anything he wants so I can stay on the course? I'd rather leave.

An image of my dad pops into my head. If I get thrown off the course, he'd be livid. But I won't give in to Leeson.

I pull myself together enough to get up from the floor, and go to a sink. I splash water on my face and rinse my mouth out to get rid of the taste of vomit. I check the mirror. I still look pale, with little blood spots around my eyes, and my hair looks limp and bedraggled, but perhaps that's a good thing given what I'm about to do.

A few minutes later I'm knocking at the door of the head of department – Dr Hargreaves, the same lady who accepted my repeated assignment.

"Come in." The voice that calls out is pleasant but decisive.

I obey. She smiles with recognition in her eyes.

"Becky White, isn't it? Are you alright, dear? Have a seat." She waves me to an orange chair opposite her and sits forward. "You don't look well."

Now I'm here, I don't really know what to say. How do I accuse one of her lecturers, a senior member of the department, of what he's just done? I have to find a way. I don't have a choice.

"Dr Leeson attacked me." It sounds incredible as the words leave my mouth.

Dr Hargreaves looks astonished and disbelieving. I don't blame her; I don't think I'd believe myself if I was listening.

"Why would you say that?" she asks.

"He threatened to have me thrown off the course if I told anyone, and I'm scared. My dad'll kill me if I get thrown off."

She looks at me steadily. There's a glisten of something in her eyes – I hope it's sympathy.

"You do know that Dr Leeson is one of our most respected lecturers, and was a barrister himself before he decided to train the next generation of this country's lawyers? No one would believe your claim."

Panic flares, and the feeling of nausea returns. What am I going to do?

"However, I think I can help you." She smiles at me, and this time there's definite sympathy in her gaze. "I will change your tutor group – you'll never need to have any direct interaction with him again. I will advise Dr Leeson not to seek any private interviews with you or any of the other female students. I will also not allow him to have you thrown off the course."

"Thank you. You're very kind. That's a huge relief," I manage a small smile back at her.

"I have the power to protect you. I would be failing in my duty if I didn't implement these measures. However, I do have a condition."

The smiles fall away; she becomes stern. My nerves return.

"It would greatly affect your credibility and career prospects if anyone were to hear of this. I am insisting that you keep quiet about this incident from now on. Do not discuss it with your friends, and do not mention it to anyone in authority. If I hear any rumours, your protected place on this course will vanish. Do we understand each other?"

I nod slowly. I don't seem to have any alternative, and silence seems a small price to pay.

"Thank you, dear. As I said, this is primarily to protect your own reputation. Who would employ a solicitor who spreads vicious rumours?" The accompanying curl of her lips carries none of the warmth of earlier.

"Who will be my new tutor?"

She consults a list and assigns me a moment later to a tutor named Dr Travers; a dragon, but at least a female one.

My timetable shows another three lectures scheduled for the day, but I can't face them. After my meeting with Dr Hargreaves, I catch one of my friends coming out of a lecture. Pleading a bad headache, I ask her to lend me her notes for today when she's finished. I've done the same for her in the past, and she agrees easily. I head to the bus stop.

Buses are frequent between the University and Halls, and it's rare to have to wait more than a few minutes for a bus. This is one of those occasions, and the bus shelter is full of students sheltering from the driving rain. There's nowhere to sit, and my legs feel as though they've been de-boned. Twenty minutes after I reach the bus stop, four buses arrive together. I get on the second one to make sure I get a seat, and rest my head against the window as it trundles its way south.

Getting off at the other end, I feel slightly better. The rain has eased a bit, and on the way back to my room I stop to check my mailbox. There's a letter from Ian – I recognise his slanty scrawl immediately from the envelope. I'm about to open it when I pause. It's not like him to write a letter. He usually sends funny postcards.

I'll open this one in private.

Chapter Twenty-Two
Tuesday 7/2/89

Daniel

I'm forcing myself to go to lectures this week. Even if I don't take much in, it's not going to help anyone if I fail my first year. This is actually a real fear, as my dad won't fund me to repeat a year, and he's too well-off for me to get a grant. This is my one chance, and I daren't blow it.

It's Tuesday, so we have a full afternoon of labs. I have to concentrate, as some of the chemicals we're using are nasty. I'm finding the work helpful. I can't think about Rick without a huge chasm opening up in my chest. It expands to fill my whole body, and threatens to swallow me. So interacting with my lab partner, a clever, sweet and shy girl named Abigail, is good therapy, as it takes me away from the chasm for minutes at a time.

I'm feeling slightly hopeful of a return to normality one day, but then I arrive back at Halls at the end of the afternoon. Deciding to go and get Becky to join me for dinner as I've not seen her all day, I take the lift up to the tenth floor. Activity on the corridor to the left draws my attention. There's a luggage trolley outside Rick's room, filled with bags and boxes. A stranger emerges from the room and starts to pick up another box. He glances in my direction, releases his hold of the box, and stands up straight.

"What are you staring at?" His tone is as aggressive as the words, and matches his general appearance: stocky build, thin mouth, and the hint of a tattoo on his neck, mostly hidden by a sweatshirt bearing a Nazi logo.

"Why are you moving in to Halls this late in the year?"

"It's got nothing to do with you, arsehole." He pauses, and picks up the box again. "Had an argument with my house mates, didn't I? They were a load of effing pricks anyway."

His swearing was less offensive to me than the tone of it. I don't blame his house mates for throwing him out (I assume that was the way it happened), but why did he have to come here? Why did he have to be the one to take Rick's room?

I turn to go and knock on Becky's door. She opens it, but seems quiet and withdrawn.

"Are you okay, Becks?"

"Fine." She pauses. "Are you okay?"

"Can I come in?"

She opens her door and stands aside, allowing me to enter. I walk over to the chair next to the desk, feeling as though something's wrong. It takes me a moment to realise.

"Oh my God, you've tidied up. Wow, well done." I smile, but the response from her is minimal; just the smallest upturn of her mouth. "Seriously, it's not like you. Is everything okay?"

"I'll be fine. I just can't talk about it; that's all."

"I thought we were friends." My voice cracks a little, as the implication that she doesn't trust me hurts more than it should.

"Of course we are." She sits on her bed and puts her hands over her face. "Something happened at Uni yesterday. I'm not allowed to tell anyone, otherwise I'll get thrown off the course, and all hell will open up and swallow me."

"Bloody hell, Becks!" I stop there. What else can I say? I wouldn't betray any confidences, but I get that maybe she's scared. "Would a hug help at all?"

The face she turns to me is tear-stained – now I come to think of it, it was like this when she opened the door to me.

"A hug would be good, thanks." She gestures for me to sit next to her on the bed, and I take my shoes off and sit by her side, wrapping an arm around her shoulder. She leans into me, and we sit in silence for a few moments, taking comfort from the closeness. I put my other arm around her, and give her a proper hug, remaining in that position, even when I feel her sobbing against me. It sets me off, and a minute later we're sobbing together; each expressing our own pain, different and yet the same. Several minutes later, she sniffs and pulls away.

"I need to blow my nose." She sounds like she has a bad cold, but it's only the tears. I hand her my clean spare hankie, and retrieve my other (less clean) one from the other pocket of my jeans. We blow our noses in unison. Despite my distress – I know the cause of this morning's tears is the invasion of Rick's room – the current situation is more sitcom than tragedy. A chuckle escapes. Becky looks at me.

"I suppose it's a bit funny. What are we like? The pair of us crying together?"

"It's what friends are for, isn't it?"

"Friends? Yes of course." Her tone is slightly off-key, and I suddenly remember that her feelings for me haven't always been platonic. We're still sitting on the bed, but facing each other now, cross-legged. The tears are more or less dried up. I'm stricken with guilt though. At this moment I wish I could change what I am, and love Becky in the way she needs to be loved – in the way she deserves to be loved.

I fidget, tying my fingers in knots. I glance at her, then move my gaze to the window. I need to be honest with her. It's not fair otherwise. I make myself look her in the face.

"Becks, I suspect you know anyway, but I kind of want to tell you."

"Tell me what?" Her tone is guarded.

"I'm gay. I was in love with Rick. I don't think he felt the same way. In fact, he pretty much threw me out when I told him. Next day he was dead."

All suspicion is gone from her face now, replaced with a painful sympathy.

"Oh God, Dan. That's awful, I'm so sorry. Not that you're gay – I mean that's fine. I'm okay with it, honestly." She smiles bravely. I can see the effort it takes, but her kindness and generosity were always going to help her through this. "But that's such a horrible way for things to end, when you never got a chance to make up with him. I'd hate for us to ever argue now."

"Me too."

"I think I understand now about why you're struggling so much with this. Do you think Alan and his group will help?"

"I don't know, but it's worth a try." Pins and needles invade my left foot, and I turn round to stretch it out. Wriggling my toes, I grimace, partly from the cramp. "We've acquired a new house-mate – if you can call him that."

"What? Oh my God. Have they been that quick? I knew they wanted the room."

"Who?"

"The University, I suppose, or whoever makes money from the rent."

"Well, I wish they'd taken the time to find someone decent."

"Why would they bother? Have you met him, Dan? Is he really awful?"

"Yeah, pretty much. Tattoos and a sweatshirt with a swastika on it. Oh, and he sounds like he's just walked off the set of *EastEnders*."

"Shit. That's not good. I'm not that fussed about the accent, or the tattoos, although I'm not keen, but a swastika! Is that even allowed?" Becky looks as horrified as I feel. My feelings of vulnerability are more often triggered by my sexuality than religion, but this definitely makes me nervous. The hairs on the back of my neck have been on high alert ever since I saw his sweatshirt.

"No idea – I don't think there are any rules about it. I don't really want to meet him again, but I guess we'll have to. Hopefully he's finished unpacking now."

She looks at her watch. "You've been here about an hour – he should be shut up in his room now, sorting out all his gear. Should we escape and grab some food?"

"Okay. There's probably not much left in the dining room now, but we could risk a pizza."

"How about getting the bus up to Rusholme and getting a curry for a change? I've not had one for ages, and I think I need a change of scenery. I've got something else to tell you as well."

She gives a grim half-smile, and we put our shoes on and head to the lifts.

As the lift arrives, the new guy turns up, and puts his foot out to prevent the doors closing. I shut my eyes for a second, in a futile attempt to shut out the image of that awful sweatshirt and its owner.

Chapter Twenty-Three
Wednesday 8/2/89

Becky

I didn't sleep last night; maybe just an hour or two. After the stress and trauma of Monday, I was sulking in my room yesterday when Dan arrived. Confirmation of him being gay wasn't a surprise, but it still hurt. Ridiculous. I should be pleased it's not personal that he doesn't fancy me. So that added to the mental torment going on in my head.

Worse, though, was the meeting with Vince, the new member of our house. Half a minute in the lift was enough to brand him as an anti-semitic, racist, homophobic idiot. Except that he's not an idiot, not really. He's frighteningly clever, and is studying politics. How do I know he's clever? The scene keeps replaying itself in my head…

He struts into the lift. He's quite a big guy; not tall, but muscular. The swastika on his pale grey sweatshirt is both offensive and scary. He looks down his nose at us.

"Sodding Jews."

"How do you know?" I can't keep my mouth shut, even when intimidated.

"What do you mean? It's effing obvious. Noses, mouths, that certain something that makes you think you're better than the rest of us."

"And you can judge that from ten seconds in a lift?"

He looks as though he's going to attack me, but just then the lift opens and a gaggle of students wait for us to leave the lift, so they can get in.

"I'm Vince. Don't forget it. Watch out for me, both of you.

Particularly the queer – I'll get him one day." He says this quietly in my ear before letting go and striding out of the lift as if nothing had happened.

On the face of it, there's nothing in this scene to make me think Vince is clever. His language and behaviour are abhorrent, and his attitudes show ignorance and prejudice. But he identified us as Jewish, and Daniel as gay, without being told. He also picked up on something which I've occasionally observed amongst my Jewish friends, although he misinterpreted it. Several of my friends have an inner confidence in their ability to achieve their goals. I don't know if it's a reaction to generations of suppression and fight for survival, or perhaps a result of close family relationships and the nurturing environment of Jewish schools, Hebrew classes and Jewish youth groups.

This is certainly not a belief in being better than anyone else. But perhaps that's how it comes across, and is the basis of some of the anti-semitism we encounter. Vince picked up on it though, which I think is both clever and frightening. I don't know what to do about it at the moment.

But the worst thing of all is the letter from Ian. In the end I couldn't bring myself to tell Dan, and it got hidden in the general discussion over the chicken korma of how awful Vince seems to be.

I drag myself out of bed, shower and dress. I can't face going downstairs for breakfast, and Dan hasn't knocked on. We parted at the lifts last night after the curry – on good terms, but I need to get my head around everything that's happened.

I nibble on left-over cold pizza as I get ready for lectures. This afternoon I'm to meet with Theresa from the self-defence class to go to see the student counsellors.

Theresa's waiting for me just inside the doors to the Students' Union. She's fiddling with the buttons on her coat, and doesn't notice me at first, as she's looking expectantly at the middle door, and I walk in through the one on the right.

"Theresa, are you okay?" I catch her attention and she gives me a small but welcoming smile.

"Hi Becky, sure. Bit nervous though. Do you honestly think this'll help?"

In truth, I don't know. Am I using Theresa as a guinea pig? Guilt flashes through me, and I feel slightly nauseous for a moment. I force a smile.

"Come on, let's get it over with." I rest my hand on her shoulder for a moment and we head to the counsellors.

We emerge after twenty minutes. Theresa's white and shaking after being made to relate all the details of her assault. The counsellor was a fairly young woman, maybe in her late twenties, with frizzy blonde hair and a bored expression. She failed to emit any sympathy, whilst extracting maximum emotion from my new friend.

I take Theresa into the bar, and sit her down in a quiet corner before providing her and me with a bottle each of Diamond White – the drink of choice for most students at the moment. I make her drink about a quarter of it before talking, and after a while the combination of cider and white wine take effect. She begins to calm down enough to talk.

"Why did I put myself through that?"

"I'm so sorry. That was my fault. I truly thought it might help."

"I know you meant well. I feel like I've been through a mangle though. That girl was such a cow. She made me go through everything in the minutest detail, only to tell me there's nothing that can be done about it. What was it she told me to do in the end? I think I was so shocked, I stopped taking it in."

"You're right she was a cow. She said you should keep quiet about it and try to forget it happened – to put it behind you."

"What would you do, Becky?" She glugs some more of her drink, lessening her shakes another notch.

"This guy, he's not your head of department or anything stupid is he?"

"No. I thought he was, but apparently he's the deputy."

"Can you ask your department head to move you to a different tutor group?"

"I suppose. What if he asks me why?"

"I guess you can either tell the truth or make something up. It's up to you. But it sounds like the only thing left is to stop it from carrying on. I guess if we can't treat it, we just have to prevent it." I know some of my frustration is creeping into my voice, but Theresa doesn't seem to notice.

"Yeah maybe. Thanks, Becky, you've been really kind. And at least we know now that the student counsellors are crap."

Oh yes! I've realised that. My options have diminished today. I'm only relieved I wasn't the one who had to confess all to the so-called counsellor.

We finish our drinks and part, with a promise to meet up at self-defence on Saturday and catch up on latest developments. I don't tell her that my latest developments are not for public knowledge.

With Ian's revelations, my options have become severely limited.

Chapter Twenty-Four
Friday 10/2/89

Daniel

The week has gone downhill, and it's all Vince's fault. Every time he passes me he shouts something offensive. I'm disgusted by being called Jewbag or Queer. The ignorance level inherent in those terms is pathetic, and – given the undercurrents of National Front propaganda – also scary and dangerous. But it was yesterday evening, on my way back from dinner in the canteen with a subdued Becky, when he took it to a new level. Becks and I had parted at the lift, ostensibly to do some studying, when I ran into Vince on my corridor. I don't know why he was there – his room is on the opposite side, facing north.

"Hey, queer-face – you been tested for AIDS yet?" Given Rick's last words to me, this cuts deep, and bile rises in my throat. I take out my key and insert it into the door, but he puts his hand out to bar my way, then steps in front of the door. "Does everyone know yet? Did Rick kill himself cos you gave him AIDS?"

"Piss off and leave me alone." A pathetic response really, but I just want to escape, and the only place I can escape to is behind him. He stands up straight, still barring my way, but looking taller and even more menacing than before. His face assumes a serious expression.

"You might want to think about copying your queer lover. If you do it in your room, no one will be able to stop you. Not like on the bridge."

"Who told you about the bridge?"

"None of your effing business." Vince jabs his finger at

my chest.

"It is my business actually. I want to know who's been talking."

"Everyone. Stupid effing prick. Did you seriously think people would shut up about the second person in the house to try to top himself? Except you failed. You can't even do that right, can you? Effing queer Jewbag. Christ, can't even get a decent group of people in Halls these days."

I'm trying to keep hold of my temper and self-control. I don't know which urge is stronger: to punch him in the face or break down in tears – neither would do me any good. But before I make a decision, Martin appears at the end of the corridor. His door is opposite mine and his room faces east.

"What's going on?" he says, his expression shocked.

"Just a bit of fooling around, mate. Can't you tell a joke when you see one?"

"It doesn't look like a joke. I would suggest you're a bit more careful. I didn't choose for you to join my house, and I would be delighted to have a reason to throw you out. Don't tempt me. Now get away from Daniel, and return to your own room. Next time I find you in this part of the building, you'll find yourself homeless."

It's the longest, and most aggressive, speech I've ever heard from Martin, and I find myself hugely grateful for his support. Vince slouches away, but the glint in his eye suggests that I've not heard the last from him yet.

I've spent the last twenty-two hours brooding over what happened. I can take Vince's taunts about my religion, though I don't like them. He's dangerous, particularly if he's part of an organised group. But I'm torn between this and horror at the similarity between him and Rick in their attitudes towards gays. Do they really think everyone who's gay has AIDS? I've not even done anything yet. And that's partly through fear of AIDS, and partly because my religious beliefs, however contradictory, prevent me from wanting to sleep around.

It is insane, because my religion also condemns homosexuality. So it would seem sensible to either accept that the religion is right, and deny my sexuality, or rebel completely against the religious ethos that denies my right to be myself.

Somehow, over the last few years, since I accepted that I'm different, I've forged a set of beliefs that tallies as much as possible with my upbringing, but loses the bits that don't suit me. Maybe this is hypocritical, but I've seen lots of other people do the same thing in their own way. A lad I was friends with in Sixth Form claimed to be religious. He wouldn't eat in other people's houses, if he didn't consider them religious enough. He occasionally caused offence by this attitude, but what I found far more offensive was his willingness to drive to football matches on Saturdays if it was a big match. He did what suited him. I do what suits me. I like to think I don't hurt anyone by my stance. Unfortunately, England in 1989 is still a hostile place for those of us who don't fit with the convention of heterosexuality. Please God, one day that will change.

Outside of the religious aspect, though, is the knowledge that Vince knows about the incident on the bridge. Was he telling the truth when he said that everyone knows, or has he wormed something out of Sanjay or one of the others? Killing myself wasn't a real option. It was a moment of insanity, brought on by grief and depression. I don't still feel like that, although the grief hasn't gone away. It tears me apart daily. I look in the mirror, and imagine Rick's with me, standing behind me or beside me, laughing at my dress sense or my musical taste – at least before his influence took hold. Or we're sitting in my room or his, discussing books or films. There are those days when I lie on my bed and daydream about us being together; what life would have been like if he'd accepted me, and if he was still alive.

The days when I can accept that he's not here any more are rare. At best, for a few moments here and there, I will face the truth, and remind myself I'll never see him again. Just for a few moments though, because then the furious monster clawing at my chest, and the bitter sting of tears in my eyes, breaks me down, and I have to curl up in a ball and protect myself before the agony of loss rips me apart.

Vince's comments have driven home to me that I can't escape this – not here, not now. I'm going to Alan's this evening, for another attempt at Friday night dinner, and a weekend in the peace and quiet of the Kabbalah house.

To my surprise, Alan has accepted that I'm gay. He's not criticised, or suggested I need to try to stop in order to get closer to Hashem. He's the first religious leader I've come across that has known and been okay with it. It's unbelievable the number of them who think I've chosen to be like this. If I could choose, why would I choose to be different? Why would I try to fit into a category of people who are condemned, avoided, and – now that AIDS is rife – feared?

So Alan's acceptance is incredible and amazing. It's made a decision for me. I'm going there this evening, and I plan to stay for the whole week if they'll have me.

I pack a couple of textbooks into my rucksack, together with enough clothes for a week, and the necessary toiletries. A sudden panic makes me wonder if it will be okay, and I go to the phone. Unbelievably there's no queue, and I dial Alan's number.

"Hello?"

"Hi Alan, it's Dan. Is it still okay for me to come up for the weekend?"

"Sure. Looking forward to seeing you."

"Thanks. Sorry, I know it's a bit cheeky, but is there any chance I could stay for the week? I'll explain when I see you."

There's a brief pause, while I panic. Have I overstepped the mark?

"Of course. Do you want me to ask Rachel to pick you up? She's over your way visiting her gran. I could give her a call, and ask her to pop in on the way. She knows where to find you."

"How come?" Why would Rachel know where I live?

There's a brief pause before Alan speaks. "I must have told her. Anyway, we discussed it last night, and she said she'd be able to pick you up, and I meant to call you, but hadn't got around to it yet. So, shall I give her a call at her gran's?"

I ignore the niggle that asks me why Alan's rambling so much in response to a simple question, and focus on the feeling of relief that I don't have to lug my overloaded and seriously heavy rucksack on the bus.

"That would be great, thanks. Can you ask her to come to my room, or Becky's if I'm not there?" I give him Becky's room number just in case. I'm not sure I can face the impatience or stress of waiting by myself.

"Alright. Time's moving on. She'll be with you in the next hour, I'd have thought."

After putting the phone down, I go and knock on Becky's door. She's apparently busy with an essay – there's a writing pad, covered in her messy scrawl, on the desk. She looks tired and fed up when she lets me in.

"I can't let you stay for long. I need to get this finished."

"It's Friday, can't it wait until the weekend?"

"I've got another two to do this weekend. I've been moved to a different tutor group, and the new tutor wants to know my strengths and weaknesses, so she's given me three long essays to do by Monday. And I've got self-defence in the morning."

"Blimey. I'll leave you to it in a minute then. I just wanted to say goodbye for now. I'm going to stay with Alan for the next week. I warned my tutor this morning that I needed a week off to deal with all the crap that's in my head right now. He was okay with it."

"Great." She hasn't sat down yet, and we're both standing in the middle of the room, looking at each other awkwardly.

"Take care of yourself, Becks. You know where I am if you need me."

"Sure. Keep in touch. Will you be able to phone me after Shabbat?"

"Course I will." I put my arms around her, and we hug fiercely for a few moments. I have a sudden horrible feeling that I won't see her again. I don't want to let her go. She's my best friend. "I mean it. You take care. Try to stay out of trouble."

She laughs, a bit shakily. "I'll do my best. You too."

Back in my room a few minutes later, I sit down to wait for Rachel. I had to duck into the common room, as I could see from the foyer that Vince was locking his door as if he was about to go out. I don't think he saw me, and as soon as I heard the lift, I escaped to the safety of my bedroom.

I'm torn now, between wanting to stay to look after Becky, who still seems to be very miserable, and a desperate need to escape from Vince for a few days. I argue with myself for a few minutes, but then there's a knock on my door. I check through the spyhole, but it's not Vince, so I open the door.

"Hi Dan. Are you ready?" Rachel walks in and gives me a brief welcome hug, before looking around. "Wow. Are you always this tidy?"

"Probably. I hate mess." I glance around, but the space is spotless except for my rucksack sitting on the chair.

"Come on then. You hate mess. I hate being late. Let's get going. The car's in the car park."

I grab my stuff and follow her to the lift. Vince can't have been away long, as he's now loitering by the phone.

"Oy, queer – off to find yourself a lover? Is she your pimp?"

My frayed temper snaps, and I punch him on the nose. I did boxing at school – mostly to prevent some of the bullying, but also to keep fit. There's a satisfying but slightly sickly crunch, and blood starts pouring from his nose.

At this point the lift arrives. Sanjay darts into the lift just as it's closing. The last I see of my tormentor is him doubled over on the floor, the flowing blood staining the carpet. Then, fortunately, the lift doors close, and I sit down and duck my head between my knees. Fainting would not go down well just now.

Arriving at Alan's house is very different from last time. The atmosphere feels welcoming and friendly, and there's a lot of laughter. Apart from Alan and Rachel, I don't recognise any of the guests. Rachel does some introductions, but then reaches an older couple, maybe in their sixties.

"I'm sorry, I don't think we've met before. I'm Rachel, and this is one of our newer members, Daniel."

"I'm Lou, and this is Jen. We met Alan last week in shul, and he invited us to come along for Friday night dinner. Always lovely to meet new people. How do you know Alan?"

"He and I have been…er… friends for about a year. We met when he moved to Manchester, and he came along to my shul. Dan just met him a few weeks ago." Rachel glosses over the circumstances, for which I'm grateful. There'll be plenty of time later for details to come out. The thought sets off butterflies, and a wave of nausea washes over me. I take a few deep breaths in an attempt to ward it off. Rachel and Lou have descended to small talk.

"Are you alright, love?" Jen is looking at me with concern.

I force a smile. "Thanks, just got a bit hot for a moment."

"That's fine. She's a pretty girl, isn't she? My Lou always had an eye for the pretty ones." She sounds remarkably calm. If my partner was eyeing someone up, I'd be livid. Not that I have a partner, but I've beheld the green-eyed monster a few times. I know the creature well. Then it dawns on me that Jen thinks I fancy Rachel. I have a few milliseconds to debate with myself whether I should tell her the truth, but decide against it for now. I've enough on my plate without coming out to a virtual stranger.

I settle for a sympathetic glance at Jen. "That's often the way." It seems to be enough, as she nods and smiles. Lou is indeed flirting with Rachel. Alan won't like that at all.

In some ways, the evening proceeds along similar lines as the last one I attended, with typical Shabbat dinner, followed by discussion in a circle, but the atmosphere is totally different. There's a lot of laughter, friendly banter and jollity.

So why does it feel as though there's about to be an explosion? Is it the dark looks Alan is sending over to Lou? Or his angry tones, as he recites grace after meals? I feel like an outside observer, watching the proceedings with a dispassionate eye. And yet occasionally I get sucked in. Jen draws me into conversation a few times at dinner, to chat about books and films – easy undemanding chatter.

A few people depart after dinner. Excuses about babysitters or elderly relatives partially placate Alan, who probably expects people to pay for their dinner by at least listening to him for a while afterwards. His demeanour sours further. There are only ten of us in the circle, including Alan, Rachel, myself, Lou (who is still obsessively dancing attendance on Rachel) and Jen (whose own sunny disposition seems to be slipping a bit). The other five – three men and two women, ranging from mid-twenties to mid-fifties in age – are otherwise friendly, interested and forthcoming.

"So, now we're settled, I'll talk about the real reason we're all here." Alan is standing up, addressing the group. He's more on edge than last time, and his tone is serious. "We're here to find Hashem. That's what Kabballah is about – searching and getting closer to Hashem; recognising that He's in our lives, and keeping Him with us." He looks around. "Sometimes it's hard. Grief, distress and difficult times can make it feel almost impossible at times, but it's my job to help every one of you achieve your Kabbalistic goals. We're each going to say what we've done this week to help us to find Hashem."

"Why don't you start off, Alan?" says Rachel. She seems tired of Lou's attention, and keen to pacify Alan.

"Okay. Thanks, Rachel." He gives her a small smile, and she seems to relax slightly. "I've put some things into place which are going to help atone for something that happened a long time ago. It's something that means a lot to me, and I'm looking forward to my plans coming to fruition." He glances around the group, seeming to make brief eye contact with everyone except me.

My brow furrows. Why is he avoiding me? And why do I have the impression that I'm somehow involved in these plans? I must be getting paranoid. I shake my head slightly, as if to get rid of the idea, and Alan turns on me. Perhaps he was watching me after all.

"Have you got something to share, Dan?"

"Not yet. Why don't we go around the circle like we did last time?"

"Because I'm in charge, and I would rather do things randomly tonight. Talk to me, what have you done to find Hashem?"

"Apart from punching someone who was offensive to Rachel and who's been upsetting me and my friends all week?"

"I'm not sure if that's quite the aim of Kabballah." Alan's tone is dry, but I'm not surprised. Even I'm not that stupid.

"No, I'm sure it's not. But it's the only thing that's happened this week to make me feel good."

"Okay. Well, maybe it's wise that you're here for the week ahead. We can work on some strategies with you."

I don't understand why this unsettles me. There's no longer an angry undertone in his voice, and his face is only showing concern. All the same, I have a weird feeling that there's more in his head than he's letting on.

Chapter Twenty-Five
Sunday 12/2/89

Becky

Dan's been gone two days, and apart from attending my self-defence class, and chatting to Theresa, I've only been out of my room to grab some food – mostly from my supplies of super-noodles from the kitchen. The essays are dragging me down, but more than that is the constant internal battle with myself.

I agreed to the deal with the department head. I still don't feel I have a choice – even less now I've seen the apathy of the student counsellors and read my brother's letter. The frustration is driving me mad though. How is it now possible to bring people like Leeson down? How many other students has he molested? Has he gone further and raped any? It doesn't seem impossible, but by keeping quiet, am I complicit in further attacks? I don't know. A call from my dad last night began with him ranting about how proud he was of me for getting into law school. It was a preliminary to the real reason for his call.

"Have you heard from Ian?" Dad's tone is a mixture of reserve, anxiety and belligerence. I guess he doesn't want to be the one to tell me the news.

"Yes, he wrote to me."

"Bloody fool." The reserve and anxiety are gone. He's just angry now. "What did he tell you?"

"He said that he'd been accused of fraud, and was being thrown out of his training post." I won't tell Dad that Ian admitted the accusation was justified. A weak moment, where it seemed easier to falsify a document than admit he'd made a mistake about a client.

"Stupid boy. He'll never get another job in law. He'll be lucky to get a job in anything. He's very lucky that I own my own business. I've told him to come and live back at home. I need another admin assistant."

"That's very good of you, Dad." I'm cautious. It's not like him to forgive misdemeanours this easily, although from what I've heard about Dan's father, mine seems easier to live with.

"I'll be keeping a close eye on him. And at least one of the admin team can give him a reference in a year or two if he wants to get an admin job somewhere else."

"I guess so."

"Anyway, Becky, I need you to get your degree, and come and join me in the business as a partner. Someone has to take over the company when I retire. I'm not planning on working forever, you know. I'm so proud of you, Becky. You got such great grades to get into Manchester. You'll do so well." Back to the proud bit. We've come round full circle. And even though he's strict and single-minded, I know how much love is behind his words. I know he's gutted by Ian's actions and the consequences. And I know that he wants me to work in the company for my security and welfare. I just wish it was for my happiness.

As soon as I get close to convincing myself to speak out against Leeson, I get knocked back. And it's the love for my dad that sways me to stay quiet, far more than any other consideration.

It's now 6pm on Sunday, and my temper is on the edge of an explosion. It'll only take a tiny spark.

Bored with noodles, and the sight of my room, I head to the lifts to go down for pizza, and maybe a bottle of cider from the off-licence. Lurking in the foyer, sitting on the stairs reading a comic of some sort, is Vince.

"Oy," he says when he sees me. "Where's your faggoty friend? Has he gone off with his pimp again?"

He looks different, and I focus on that for a moment to stop myself from killing him – self-defence has advanced to include pressure points, and I reckon I could give it a good go now. This guy is really annoying me. Why doesn't he mind his own business? Nosy bugger…

His nose. That's what's different. It's crooked.

"What happened to your nose?"

"Your effing friend has got an effing vicious left hook. If I see him again, he's dead. I'd take it out on you, but he's not here to witness it."

"I am, though, and if you touch Becky, you'll get a lot more than a broken nose." Greg emerges from the common room looking tough and angry.

Vince mutters something and rolls up his comic – which I can now see is the latest copy of *Viz*. Probably the one that was on the common room windowsill yesterday when I popped in for a moment to see if there was anyone to chat to. He heads away from the lifts in the direction of his room.

Greg turns to me, a friendly grin on his face. "That seems to have got rid of him. Do you fancy coming for a drink?"

"I was thinking about some food, to be honest."

"Come on then. Do you like Chicago Diner? We can get the bus down to Withington. Maybe catch a film or something." He raises his eyebrows in a question.

"That sounds great. I'm a bit scruffy though. Should I get changed?"

"You look pretty good to me, Becky." He looks me up and down, and my temperature rises about ten degrees in a millisecond. If he's okay with my t-shirt, jeans and sweatshirt, then I'll have to go with it, even if it's not what I'd have planned to wear on a date. Although maybe I'm getting ahead of myself.

Dinner's over, and there was nothing on at the pictures that we fancied. Greg invited me for a drink instead, and we're now in the Queen of Hearts downing Diamond White like it's about to be rationed.

After two bottles, I'm feeling a bit light-headed, and get a bit giggly when he moves across the seat until his thigh is pressing against mine.

"You're really sexy, you know that?" he mutters in my ear. I didn't know, but I'm not going to argue.

I turn my face to him, and before I have time to think, his tongue is probing my mouth. Sensations compete for attention throughout my body, and I want him more than I've ever wanted anyone. I'm still a virgin, but suddenly the reason why escapes me. I've got this hot guy kissing me senseless, and all I want right now is him.

He finally pulls back, and I feel bereft for a minute, until he says, "Let's get out of here. Back to my room, okay?"

I nod and we finish our drinks quickly, then hurry back to Halls. The fresh air fails to dampen my ardour, and the rapidly-downed drinks outweigh any benefits from the fresh air. By the time we get to his room, I'm well past tipsy.

I barely remember losing my virginity, but wake up in his bed, sore and naked, and with a pounding head. I pull myself together enough to notice the used condom in his bin. Thank goodness I retained enough sanity to insist on that. With the risk of AIDS so prevalent in the news, I'd have been stupid not to. Let alone the fear of pregnancy. I throw on some clothes while he watches me, and dive out of the room and round to the girls bathrooms to throw up.

After a short while I return to his corridor, and knock on the door.

"You look a bit of a wreck, doll. Maybe sleep it off a bit, and we'll catch up again tonight."

I nod and wince, then check my watch.

No chance of sleeping it off – I've got a tutorial to get to.

Chapter Twenty-Six
Wednesday 15/2/89

Daniel

I've been here five full days now, but feel no closer to getting to know Alan.

Only Rachel and I stayed over on Friday night, and it's obvious that she and Alan are sleeping together; not that I'd had doubts particularly. Rachel remains friendlier to me than Alan does. He ranges from being friendly, kind and sympathetic one day, to surly and uncommunicative the next.

His mood improved on Friday as soon as Lou and Jen left. He talked well into the early hours of Saturday morning, telling tales from the Torah to Rachel and me, as we curled up in armchairs in the centrally-heated private lounge.

Some twenty or so people joined us on Saturday morning, for further Kabbalistic discussion and a proper Shabbat morning service. I'm getting more accustomed to the ideas of Kabballah. A lot of people talk about mysticism, and perhaps there is something a bit mystical about the idea of getting close to God. But it doesn't feel as strange as it sounds. I decided a few years ago that I would dictate what I believe in, and that my God doesn't condemn me for what I am. How could He create people as homosexuals, and then censure them for being as He created them? It makes no sense. What is more likely is that fear and prejudice have helped to spread contempt. Religious leaders have found it easier to accept heterosexuality, so they've preached hatred for what they don't understand.

Alan confuses me sometimes with his moodiness, but I'm grateful for his acceptance, and lack of judgement, even if

I'm not ready to come out to the wider group yet.

Since the end of Shabbat, Alan's split his time between his own work, and re-teaching me Hebrew. I've forgotten most of what I learned for my Bar Mitzvah, which was over five years ago.

Rachel has been in and out of the house. She seems to have her own key, and always arrives in time for dinner and stays until after breakfast. I guess she's reconciled it with her dad somehow. Sunday she was here some of the day as well, but she works full time, and is currently out of the house.

It's now Wednesday morning, eleven-thirty. I've put aside my Hebrew for this morning, while Alan's busy with his own concerns, and I'm working at the dining table alone, writing up an experiment from last week on extraction of DNA. At least, I'm trying to. I keep getting distracted by thoughts of Rick. Was there anything left in his bedroom that day that could confirm if someone else was there? Would they be able to one day find a hair lying around, and use the DNA to convict someone? A lecture last week suggested that would be possible, and probably very soon. Would they find my DNA? Would I be a suspect? Or is there nothing to find, and Rick just killed himself?

So many questions. I can't bring myself to ask the next one – the obvious question that leads on from the suicide. Because if someone asks 'Why?', would the answer be 'Extreme disgust and fear at his gay friend's confession' or perhaps worse: 'Extreme disgust at being kissed by a guy, and fear of AIDS as a result?'? Are they sufficient reasons to take one's own life?

"Why aren't you studying your Hebrew?" Alan's voice comes from the doorway, loud and accusatory.

"Sorry, Alan. I had some work to finish for Uni."

"I thought you weren't going back this week?" He sounds angry.

"I've got things to hand in at my tutorial next Monday." I blench a little at the fury in his expression. "I'll get back to my Hebrew now. Sorry."

"Good. I can't spend every minute of the week with you,

you know. Kabbalah isn't easy. You have to practise, and the first steps are to familiarise yourself with the Torah. To do that, you need to learn Hebrew."

"I've not forgotten everything. I'm just a bit out of practice."

"Well then, get back in practice. Most of the members would love to have a week spare to study Hebrew and Torah – it's not a privilege granted to many people in this day and age. Everyone is too busy. If my twin had been able to do this, he might still be alive now."

He turns and slams the door behind him before I get a chance to ask about his brother. He's mentioned him a few times now, but apart from a tacit reminder that he committed suicide, I've been able to find out nothing. I don't really dare to ask questions. As soon as the subject comes up – always through Alan's own comments – he changes the subject immediately. It's like these comments escape occasionally because he can't keep them in, but he refuses to dwell on them. But his brother's suicide might explain why Alan turned to Kabbalah.

I push aside my half-finished report, and pick up the Hebrew book I put on the shelf after breakfast.

I return to studying after a light lunch of cheesy scrambled eggs. Alan didn't speak much during lunch, but he seemed less angry. I'm looking forward to Rachel coming back. She seems able to coax him back into a good mood.

I hear the front door slam a short while after lunch. Alan didn't tell me he was going out, but he's under no obligation to do so – it's his house, and I'm just a guest, and probably an unwanted one at that.

It's gone four when I hear the door open again.

"Dan?" Alan shouts from the direction of the hall. "Can you come and give me a hand?"

I go into the hall, and see him struggling to bring several plastic bags into the house.

"There are more in the car, Dan. Can you grab a few, and bring them in?"

"Sure." I go outside, shivering as the bitter February wind cuts mercilessly through my sweatshirt. There are six carrier bags in the open boot. I peek inside one, to see DIY-type supplies, such as masking tape, a Stanley knife, and several coils of rope. Footsteps on the pavement alert me, and I grab three of the bags and haul them out of the boot and up the garden path. As I pass Alan, I give him a brief smile.

"I'll grab the last ones and shut the boot. Empty the bags onto the dining room table, will you?"

I nod, and lug the bags past him into the dining room where I've been working. I pile my work neatly onto a chair, and start emptying the bags, one by one.

In addition to the items previously noted, I extract a sheaf of paper, blankets, a pillow and a bucket. There are several tins of soup, some spoons, and a plastic water bottle, of the kind athletes use.

I stack the items as neatly as possible on the table, and wait for Alan to return. He comes in a couple of minutes later, but he's empty-handed.

"I changed my mind. Can you put everything in the kitchen? Bring it through. I've got some preparation to do while you carry on with your reading." His tone is strange. Not angry exactly, but nonetheless it gives me sudden chills.

Chapter Twenty-Seven
Thursday 16/2/89

Becky

I dragged myself to the phone on Tuesday to call in to Uni. It's not hard to fake a bad cold, particularly after crying all night.

So why have I been crying? Is it because Greg's turned out to be a selfish sod? He got what he wanted on Sunday night, and then dumped me after lectures on Monday.

I knocked on his door as soon as I got back on Monday, ready to ask him to join me for dinner in the canteen. He opened the door with a towel round his waist.

"What do you want? I'm not alone."

"Who is it, Greggy? Is it that dim cow you were talking about? The frigid virgin?" The sneer in the girl's voice was almost as bad as the words. Greg had clearly lost no time in slagging me off to his newest girlfriend.

I ran back to my room, all thoughts of eating gone. Locking my door behind me, I sat and brooded about the stupidity of throwing myself away on a selfish, womanising bastard.

The books and magazines never quite portrayed how awful the pain could be. For the last two years I've read every copy of *Cosmopolitan* from cover to cover, and there was no clue that it would be like this. It's now early on Thursday morning and I'm lying curled up on my bed, for the hundredth time since Monday evening. My period has begun, which I'm sure hasn't helped the pain – a delightful combination of 'just lost virginity' and 'worst period pain cramps ever'. If I could face the kitchen I'd go and fill a hot water bottle, but I dread the thought that he's been spreading rumours around the whole floor, or maybe even the whole Tower. I settle for dragging myself off the bed, and downing a couple of paracetamol.

I check my watch. Six-thirty. I've got no lectures until eleven this morning. I try to catch another couple of hours sleep. It's unlikely the kitchen would be busy at this time of day, but just in case. And anyway, I really need to sleep.

The last few days have been a weird mix of anger, hurt pride, physical pain and worrying about Ian. I can't sort anything out in my head – it's all a jumble. I wish Dan was here to talk to. He wouldn't judge me.

I wake up at ten, and replay the same old arguments in my head. I genuinely believed that Greg liked me. Was he just using me for sex? It seems likely now. But why would he do that if he could get that bimbo to join him only a day later? I spend a few minutes swearing at my bedraggled reflection in the mirror. It didn't take long for me to realise I've only myself to blame. I turned to Greg because I've been missing Dan. I allowed him to get me drunk that first night, when I responded clumsily enough to his embraces to end up in his bed, losing my virginity. When I self-analyse really deeply, it occurs to me that my dad's approval might be mixed up in this, in a complicated sort of way. I sit down, and try to work it out.

Dad has always told me to save myself for 'the one', and preferably until I get married. So his recent attempts to dictate to me have stirred up a rebellion. I don't feel able to stand up to Leeson and dump my course, so perhaps the easier way to rebel against my dad is a stupid one-night stand.

On the other hand, I could have just been feeling lonely, and getting drunk led me into the bed of that pig. I've given up even thinking his name. He's not worth it.

I drag myself to the bathroom. Dressed, and looking halfway-decent (if you discount the pale face and dark-ringed eyes), I make my way to the lifts, ready to head to Uni for a lecture with the dreaded Leeson. I may not have him for tutorials any more, but I can't avoid his lectures.

Vince is lurking outside the lifts, sitting on the stairs with that blasted comic again. I swear that bloke sits in wait to torment me.

"Oy, slut – I hear that Greg's not going to be protecting you again. Do you want to know what he's been saying about you?"

"No. Go away." I push the button for the lift, pressing it several times in the vain hope it'll come along more quickly.

"I'll have you. I don't mind other blokes' leftovers. Come on. I'll even fuck a Jewish bitch if I have to." He reaches out as if to grab me, but my fists move quickly, twisting upwards and knocking Vince's greedy hands away from me. I sidestep him as the lift arrives, and step quickly inside, thankful there are three other girls and a male tutor inside.

It's a struggle inside the lift to keep it together. Now I've escaped from Vince, it feels as though every straight male on the planet is out to molest me. I know that's an exaggeration, but I don't feel safe any more. My body has been violated, even though I technically gave my permission, and now everyone seems to want a piece. I want to scream, or cry, or swear, or something.

"Are you okay?" one of the girls says. She's looking at me with a curious sort of sympathy.

I manage a half smile and nod. "Thanks."

It's a relief when the lift stops on the ground floor, and I dive quickly out of the building, run across the road at the pedestrian crossing and jump on to the bus as it's about to leave. Anonymity. A lot of elderly folk heading into Manchester for a day's shopping probably, or maybe up to the Infirmary for an appointment or two. All safe anyhow. Perhaps I need to immerse myself in life to take my mind off everything.

Friday 17/2/89

After a restless night, I'm woken by a knock on my bedroom door. I scramble out of bed, and peek through the spyhole. Martin is standing there with a couple of strangers – a man and a girl.

I open the door with the chain still across and speak through the crack.

"Can you give me a few minutes please?"

"Of course, Becky. This is Mr and Miss Ledermann – Daniel's father and sister. We'll wait for you in the common room."

Ten minutes later, I'm clean and dressed. I walk to meet Dan's family with some trepidation. Why do they want to see me?

"Hi. Sorry to keep you waiting. I didn't sleep well, so I overslept." I'm rambling again. These visitors don't need to know about my problems.

The man stands up, and I can see a faint resemblance to Dan, but just in the nose and the shape and colour of the eyes. He's taller than Dan, with greying hair and a seeming inability to smile. He doesn't offer to shake hands.

"Where's my son? Your tutor says you might know."

"He's gone to stay with some friends in North Manchester for a few days. I'm sure he's fine."

The girl, Dan's sister according to Martin, looks relieved. She keeps a slight distance from her dad, and I see her cast him a wary glance as I finish speaking. I know from Dan that she's fifteen, shy and clever. She has a sweet face, and I'd much prefer to chat with her than with her father.

"What would you know?" Mr Ledermann goes over to the window, and stares out for a moment before rounding on me. Martin is guarding the door of the common room. From the corner of my eye, I see him turn away a couple of students.

"What do you mean? Dan's my friend."

"Some friend. You drove him to attempt suicide. Why would you care?"

"What? He didn't attempt suicide – not really. It was a misunderstanding and a mistake. He never intended to go through with it."

"You're a blithering idiot. No wonder my son tried to top himself if you're his only friend." This man is not listening to me. My temper rises – I only have a fragile hold on it at the moment anyway. "I know about suicide. A young man I was doing business with. Tragic really, but there was nothing I could have done. I made an effort to learn the signs though. It's important to understand how far someone can be safely pushed."

I raise my eyebrows. I can't help it. Does he realise how he just came across?

"Dan's safe at the house of a friend – a religious leader who'll look after him, and is very concerned about his mental welfare."

He makes a harrumphing sound, and looks down his nose at me.

Martin leaves his place by the door and comes over to us.

"Becky, why don't you look after Daniel's sister for a while? I need to speak to Mr Ledermann for a short while in my room. You're not rushing off to lectures are you?"

"No, I'm fine. I'll be happy to stay and chat to Dan's sister." I turn to her. "Sharon, isn't it? Shall we sit down?"

She nods, and I guide her to a couple of comfy chairs by the window, as Martin leads her dad from the common room. I pray that Greg or Vince won't walk in, but will have to trust to luck for now that they're both at lectures or asleep.

"Do you really think Daniel's okay?" Sharon moves a thick strand of long straight black hair out of her eyes and tucks it behind her ear. She resembles Dan more than her dad does, with the same-shaped face and the same generous mouth. She seems kind and anxious. I want to reassure her, but I haven't actually heard from Dan since he left last Friday, and when I tried to call yesterday evening, the phone rang out. I gave up after about twenty rings. I tried again an hour later, but with the same effect. It was a Thursday evening, so they might have gone out somewhere, but I have a niggle.

"I'm hoping to catch up with him later today before Shabbat comes in. He's supposed to be back on Sunday, but things haven't been great around here for the last week or two." I hesitate, and glance at Sharon. She's looking at me with concern in her eyes. "You know about Rick?"

"Daniel wrote to me. I wanted to answer, but Dad's been vetting my mail, and there's no post box near the school. It's hard to slip out without him noticing."

"Why wouldn't your dad want you to write to Dan?"

"It's a long story, but Dad's really angry with him for raising the possibility of suicide. This is kind of a reaction to that. There's also the thing about him being gay. Daniel tried to come out once. It was shortly after Mum passed away, and Dad went ballistic. In the end, he told Daniel it was just a phase and that he'd 'better grow out of it'. Dad checks my letters to make sure I'm not encouraging 'that nonsense'."

"So what do you know about Rick?"

"I read between the lines of Daniel's letter to me. He knows that he can't say things outright, but he said that Rick was a close friend, and that he'd got a bit freaked out when Daniel was totally honest with him. It was something like that anyway. I can't remember the exact words. Anyway, it was pretty obvious that my brother tried coming out to Rick – I think maybe he fancied Rick – and it went horribly wrong. The next time Daniel saw him, he was dead."

"Bloody hell. That's worse than I thought."

"Shh." Sharon puts her finger to her lips. There are footsteps coming down the corridor, and a second later her dad appears with Martin. Mr Ledermann looks angry, frazzled and uncomfortable.

I try to ease the tension. "Are you staying in Manchester tonight?"

"No." Mr L snaps at me.

"We drove up early this morning. Dad's got a business meeting at three, so we have to be back in Birmingham by then." Sharon puts her hand out. "It was lovely to meet you, Becky. I know you'll do your best to help Dan."

"Thanks, Sharon. Always. And it was nice meeting you too."

A few minutes later, they're gone. Martin looks at me apologetically.

"There's still time for some breakfast if we're quick." He

smiles invitingly. After all that's happened, he's one of the few men I still trust.

"Sounds good. I think I need some food." I glance at my watch. Ten-fifteen.

The lifts are quick. Most people are at lectures. I'm late now, but this is more important. I need to find out what Dan's dad said to Martin, and also ask if there's a way I can get Greg and Vince kicked out. Maybe that's childish, but I don't think I can face either of them any more.

Chapter Twenty-Eight
Thursday 16/2/89

Daniel

Where am I? A banging headache, dizziness and feeling sick add to the general disorientation. I open my eyes a fraction more than a slit. Complete darkness.

What? What's going on? My throat constricts with the sudden panic. I open my eyes wide. Still nothing. What if I never see again? What's happened? And where the hell am I?

I try to quell the panic by re-tracing my last steps before I got here. I was unloading shopping. Weird things. Alan was behaving strangely. I watched him pour some liquid onto a dishcloth. He came over to me.

Then I woke up here with this awful headache and no vision. I'm still wearing a sweatshirt and jeans – I can feel the fabric against me. My pulse is still racing. I'm blind. Is it permanent? WHY CAN'T I SEE?

I feel around me. I'm sitting on a cold hard floor – concrete. There's nothing within reach. Maybe it's just too dark here, and I'm not blind after all – I turn my head to the side. My world spins – a weird sensation when I can't actually see. I allow it to settle for a moment, staying completely still but remaining upright.

What the hell am I going to do? I can explore the area with my hands and other senses. Why am I dizzy? That dishcloth. What was that liquid? It must have knocked me out. Chloroform? Shit. Why would Alan use chloroform to drug me? Why the hell would he do this?

I shiver. I try to convince myself it's from the cold, rather than fear. But I'm bloody terrified. Ignoring it doesn't seem to be helping. I want to howl out loud, but that's scary too. What consequences might that have? I daren't think about it. What's happened? The only thing I know is that Alan did this. Why? What have I done to upset Alan so much? This is not normal.

I force myself to trawl back through my memory, despite wincing from the shooting pains in my head. But there's no enlightenment. I'm completely in the dark – in every sense.

A creaking sound causes the back of my neck to tingle. There's a faint glow – perhaps I'm not completely blind – but I can't see anything else.

"So you're alive." Alan's voice is the only indication that anyone's in the room with me. It seems to have come from the left, so I twist around to face the source. The room spins again – an added dimension with the glow as it bobs and fades for a second before settling down.

"Yeah, I think so. What happened?"

"You hit your head when you fell. The combination of the chloroform and the head injury knocked you out more than I intended. It seems to be roughly the same place that got injured in the snow when we met."

"Why would you use chloroform on me? What have I done to you?"

"We'll come to that later. How's your head?"

I put my hand to the back of my head – the likely source of the pain. It's wet and sticky. For a brief moment I'm relieved I can't see my hand. Only for a moment though. Fear that I might be permanently blinded prevents me from speaking for a while, and it's Alan who breaks the silence.

"You seem weird. Why aren't you looking at me?"

I toy with the idea of lying. It could be useful to hide the fact that I can't see. Maybe I would seem less vulnerable. I don't think I could carry it off though.

"I can't see properly. Only the glow of the light."

"You must have done some damage when you fell then. Chloroform shouldn't cause blindness."

"I still don't get why you'd need to use chloroform on me. What's going on? Where am I?"

"I didn't think you'd come down to my cellar of your own accord. It seemed the easiest way to get you here." His matter-of-fact tones are almost more chilling than if he sounded angry. I remember now bringing the items through to the kitchen, and he had the same normal tones then, although they somehow conveyed that there was something going on. I just had no idea what then. I'm still no wiser now.

"Have I done something to upset you, Alan?"

"Not exactly. You'll find out more in due course. You'll not be getting out of here for a while – if ever. Plenty of time for you to hear the full story. Anyway, you'd better be quiet. Guests for dinner will be arriving soon. If there's any indication of noises in my cellar, I'll come down and gag you. If you want to remain free, stay quiet. I'll bring you some food when everyone's gone."

"What about Rachel?"

"What about her?"

"Won't she wonder where I am?" My heart hammers in my chest. Perhaps I should have kept quiet and prayed for her to rescue me.

"Hmm, good thinking. Maybe she would. Perhaps I'd better not let her stay tonight." There's something strange in his tone, and I wonder if I've angered him. He was furious last week with Lou's flirting. But now he sounds more amused than angry. I can't work it out, so let it go for now. "There are pillows and blankets in the corner. I'll let you find them for yourself though. It'll give you something to do. Just keep quiet. Oh, and there's a bucket in another corner. Try not to wet yourself finding it. I'll give you a clue. It's the opposite side of the room to the door."

"Thanks." I don't know why I'm thanking him. For pointing me in the direction of the bucket? For providing blankets and pillows? For not killing me? Maybe all three. Maybe because politeness might keep me alive long enough for someone to rescue me.

I listen as the door creaks shut, then identify the sound of a key in a lock. Perhaps my other senses are becoming more acute to compensate for the lack of sight.

Oh God, please let me see again. Please get me out of here alive! Send someone to rescue me, or give me the strength and tools to rescue myself.

Please, God, I'm sorry if being gay has offended you. Perhaps it's not part of your plan. But please, please forgive me. I need you to help me. Please.

Chapter Twenty-Nine
Friday 17/2/89

Becky

Martin takes a seat at the edge of the dining room where it's relatively quiet.

"Get yourself some food, Becky. I had breakfast at seven this morning, so I'm not hungry."

Armed with toast, grapefruit and orange juice on a tray, I join the house tutor a few minutes later.

"I'm concerned about Daniel," he says. "Some of things his father told me suggest he might still be suicidal."

"He was never suicidal, not really. He had a bit of a wobble in the launderette, and got into some sort of a trance. He woke up to find himself on that bridge. As soon as he realised where he was, he wanted to get down, but that stupid policeman didn't give him a chance to explain."

"Daniel's father suggested that his son has… er… homosexual tendencies."

"Dan's gay, yes. That has nothing to do with suicide though." Although if he was in love with Rick, the events that unfolded after Dan's confession could well have contributed to suicidal tendencies. But Martin doesn't need to know that.

Wincing at the blunt response, Martin continues: "Mr Ledermann has had some experience with suicide, and would like to be certain that his son won't go down that route. He feels that Daniel's… er… homosexuality makes him vulnerable. To be honest with you, and I probably shouldn't tell you this, but I felt that Mr Ledermann's attitudes towards his son could be a significant factor in any depressive tendencies that Daniel might have."

"We can agree on that. The man is horrible." I manage to extract a small, if somewhat guilty, smile from Martin. I can't argue that Dan's depressed. I've seen plenty of signs of it, but then he's got plenty to be depressed about. "Did the police ever discover whether Rick committed suicide, or if it was…" I tail off – saying 'murder' to Martin seems a step too far. I don't think he could handle it.

"There's been no further information. I do know that his parents arranged for his body to be transferred to their home town. The funeral was yesterday, but his parents wanted it to be a quiet event with just family. I only found out yesterday evening that it had taken place." His brow draws together in furrowed lines. "I think it was unfair of them to exclude his student friends, but it's their prerogative."

"We need to discover what actually happened, don't we? Otherwise, there'll be people that blame themselves, or even that are under suspicion by the police."

"I believe the police are convinced that it's suicide. The inquest was adjourned, but the police inspector, DI Bannister, said it was most likely they would bring in a verdict of suicide when the full inquest takes place."

"They'll settle for most likely? That's outrageous. What about the burden of guilt it places on his friends? They'll have to live with that."

Martin reacts to my outburst with a look of sympathy, and touches my hand gently for a second. "Which is worse, do you think: guilt or suspicion?"

"What do you mean?"

"Is it worse to feel guilty for possibly causing someone's suicide, or to be under suspicion for actually killing someone?"

I eat some toast in silence for a moment, using the chewing time to think.

"The best solution is to find out who did it and why, and get them arrested."

"As long as you get the right person."

"Thanks, Martin." I hesitate, wondering whether to bring

up the subject of Vince and Greg.

It's as if he's read my mind. "I heard you're having some troubles of your own, Becky. I've also used my eyes and ears and I'm working on the removal of Vince from the house. His views and behaviour are unacceptable. It's been reported to the University, but there's a lot of bureaucracy to work through. In the meantime, do your best to avoid him, and also the other young man. Remember the old saying, *Sticks and stones may break my bones, but words will never hurt me*."

I try to conjure a smile, but fail. "No offence, but the old saying stinks." I pick up my tray and stand up. "Thanks anyway."

He stands up too, takes the tray from me, and carries it to the trolley by the door. The chivalry seems odd in the circumstances, but perhaps Martin is trying to show by his actions that not all men are traitorous bastards. We return to the tenth floor in near silence, but it's companionable. Parting at the lifts, I thank him again for his help and advice.

"Thank you too, Becky. And please keep an eye out for Daniel. I'd be grateful if you could let me know when he returns, or if you speak to him. I'm getting a little bit worried."

He's not the only one. I go to my room to grab my things for Uni, the phone number Dan gave me for Alan, and a pile of 10p pieces for the phone. I have to wait for the phone to be free, and return to my room, emerging three times before I can finally use it. My hand shakes as I try again to call the number, but there's still no reply.

A niggle gnaws in my stomach.

Saturday 18/2/89

The next day, I drag myself to self-defence. I'm feeling very ambiguous about it at the moment. It saved me from Leeson and Vince, but it couldn't save me from myself. But that's not a good enough reason to ditch it, and anyway, I'm keen to see Theresa. She was chatty last time I saw her, but hadn't been able to change anything as she'd had a stomach bug and missed Uni on the Thursday and Friday.

I catch up with her outside the building.

"Hi, Theresa, how are you doing?"

"Great thanks. I've got everything sorted."

"Brilliant." I brush aside the faint irritation that she didn't ask how I am, but as I had no intention of telling her the truth, perhaps this is better. "What happened?"

She guides me into a quiet corner so we can chat as we get ourselves ready for the class.

"My tutor asked me to stay behind after class on Thursday. I waited until everyone had gone, then said, 'I'm not carrying on with this. Either you promise to stop, or I'm going to ask to move tutor groups, and I'll tell them why.' He looked really shocked. I mean, he was just silent for like, I don't know, maybe two whole minutes. Then he said, 'Okay, you win. I'll keep my hands to myself, even though it's torture not to touch you, you're so beautiful. But you have to promise me not to tell anyone.' I suppose I was a bit flattered at being called beautiful, so I just agreed, but I can't help wondering if I should have done more really."

"I don't know how much more you could have done. I'm still not entirely happy that I've accepted a deal from my course head, but at least I don't have to go near that disgusting piece of work again – the tutor, not the course head."

"Well, I wish I didn't have to go near my tutor again, but he's forbidden me from speaking to anyone about it, so I'll have to see how it goes."

At this point, we're called through to start the class, and as I practice key moves from Jiu-Jitsu, I wonder if I'll have to use it again. I much prefer confining my new skills to class.

Chapter Thirty
Saturday 18/2/89

Daniel

I wake up to the sound of the key in the door. Fear grips me. Any trust for Alan has disappeared. He's trapped me here, and hinted I may never escape. The hairs prickle on the back of my neck. I wrap the blankets around me more tightly. I eventually managed to locate them on Thursday as the temperature dropped from chilly to freezing.

It took me a long time of crawling around the room on my hands and knees, feeling around the floor every few inches. I found the bucket first and used it, the need to empty my bladder having given me the original impetus to move. Clumsy with lack of sight, I nearly knocked it over, but more by luck than judgement, managed to catch it before it fell, and I set it with care against the wall, feeling my way. I then edged along with the bucket, until I reached a corner of the room. I lodged the bucket in the exact corner for ease of locating it again next time. Then resumed my search, this time for the bedding that Alan had promised.

At some point in the search, I got disorientated, and found myself back at the bucket. I decided to be more logical, and instead of heading randomly into the centre of the room, I felt my way around the walls, always keeping a wall on my left. That way, I couldn't get lost. If I found myself back at the damn bucket again with no blanket, I'd have had to take a different approach, but Alan had left the bedding in a corner as he'd said.

I didn't sleep well, alternating with worries about the physical discomforts, my lack of sight, and why the hell I'm here. I'm not used to sleeping on a concrete floor. I'm also more accustomed to duvets and sheets than a single scratchy blanket and a flat smelly pillow. Alan must have kept the new one for himself, as the one I've been left smells of his aftershave and sweat. In the short space of time that I've been here, any liking I had for him has turned to hate. How could he do this to me?

I lay awake for hours, trying to keep warm. The house's central heating hasn't extended to this cellar. I don't even know how long I've been here.

By the time the key creaks in the lock, I'm feeling exhausted: my eyes are gritty, my head is foggy, and I'm feeling bruised and achey. Adding in my sore head, which hasn't had sufficient time to heal since Alan left, and the only positive is that the exhaustion is numbing some of the fear.

The glow is a bit brighter this time, and I can dimly make out a vague human shape.

"Good morning, Dan." Alan's voice is bright and cheerful.

"What's good about it?"

"Ooh, someone's grumpy."

"You'd be grumpy if you'd had to sleep on a hard floor in winter with a single blanket, not to mention I can't actually see. And I still don't know why you're keeping me here. I don't know what day it is, and I'm hungry." I hadn't meant to admit that, but my rumbling stomach is reminding me I've not eaten for many hours – not since Wednesday's breakfast.

"Just as well I've brought you food then. It's Shabbat morning, so you're in luck." There's a rustling of paper, the shape comes closer to me, and a soft round bun is pressed into my hand. It smells of challah bread, and is likely one of the prayer rolls that was left over from last night's dinner. I'm grateful for it though.

"Thanks." I start to eat it hurriedly, afraid that he'll take it away before it's finished.

"Slow down. It's not healthy to eat that fast. You might choke."

I stop eating for a second and take a deep breath, forcing myself not to respond. So many things I'd like to say – none of them wise. I resume eating, more slowly this time. I finish, but my throat is now dry.

"Please could I have something to drink?"

"Of course you can. I'm not an ogre. I'm not here to starve you to death. Not yet."

Not yet? What the hell does that mean?

He presses a bottle into my hands. It's cold. I feel for the top and unscrew the lid. I bring the rim to my lips and tilt it gently. Cool water fills my mouth. I drain the bottle, unsure if I'd be allowed to keep it, but wanting to hydrate myself as much as possible while I've got the chance. I put the empty bottle next to me.

"What are you planning to do with that?" His tone sounds amused and curious.

"I don't know, but I can't see you to give it back."

"Hold it out and I'll take it from you."

I do as I'm told, but feel strangely bereft as he takes the bottle from me, even though I hadn't formulated a use for it. Maybe I could have weed into it if I couldn't be bothered to go to the bucket every time? The idea makes me feel slightly nauseous. Perhaps it's as well that I had to give it back.

"Why am I here?"

"Because I need you to be. Your father owes me a debt. You're going to pay it for him."

"What debt?"

"It's a long story, and I've got things to do. My followers will be here shortly for the next meeting. Not that I'm really a Kabbalistic leader, but it amuses me to watch them all." He laughs, and the hairs on the back of my neck tingle again. "Bye for now, Dan. See you later. Try to get some sleep. It might make you less grumpy."

I don't reply, just wait for him to leave and lock the door behind him. As the lock grates, I wonder how long it will be before I get anything else to eat or drink.

At what point did I stop wondering if I'll be set free? Probably when Alan mentioned my dad.

I know my dad could be ruthless sometimes in his business practices, as well as in his dealings with his family.

He was always strict with us. He'd say it was for our own good, but I don't think he knows how to be kind. When Mum died, we lost all parental love. I don't think Dad even cared that she'd gone. He settled quickly into a routine, leaving us to obey his rules but to otherwise fend for ourselves while he worked.

He spent more time at home, working from the Amstrad computer and the phone in the spare room. Sharon and I split all the chores between us, making sure that cooking, cleaning and laundry got sorted out between homework. Any mess was severely frowned upon, and untidy or dirty surfaces still send chills through me. Dad wouldn't shout particularly – but the tone of disgust in his voice, and the occasional clip around the ear if he was properly angry, made sure we both knew that certain behaviours weren't tolerated.

I don't know what made me think it was okay for me to come out. There was a documentary on telly about AIDS. Dad was sitting with us after dinner for a rare family hour. He started spouting nonsense about 'all these disgusting gays sleeping with everyone. They deserve all they get.'

"Not all gays are promiscuous," I said. "I'm gay, and have no intention of sleeping around."

Dad's reaction was predictable: "Forget such rubbish. No son of mine could be that vile." Then he sent me straight to my room.

He never directly mentioned it again, and neither did I, but it became apparent that he was keeping a closer watch on my and Sharon's activities. I don't think he wanted me to go to University, but as he's too well-off for me to get a student grant, I think he felt able to control me with threats of financial destitution if I 'misbehaved'. The threats have been subtle and discreet, but I'm astute enough to understand the underlying message in every letter – '*Funds will be made available, contingent on you working hard and behaving appropriately*'. This sentence has been the conclusion of each of his monthly letters that he's sent to me. Becky's the only other person I know who doesn't get a grant, but I'm sure her dad wouldn't dream of cutting off the funding.

Sharon's total lack of anything controversial in her correspondence has indicated that Dad is almost certainly vetting all letters.

So, returning to the key question: what did Dad do to Alan? And how am I supposed to 'repay the debt'?

Chapter Thirty-One
Monday 20/2/89

Becky

Another Monday, so I'm sitting as far back in the lecture theatre as possible, waiting for Dr Leeson to arrive. The subject is conveyancing law, not my favourite anyway. I've managed to avoid him since changing tutor groups, but Rosanna, one of the girls in his group, said he was furious the other day when I didn't turn up. Apparently the head of department forgot to inform him of my move.

As he enters, he glances around the room. I duck my head a little lower, hoping that the head of the tall law student in front blocks me from view, but the theatre is a little too well-tiered for my liking.

"Miss White – I need to see you after class. Come to my office."

"I'd rather not."

"Excuse me?" He sounds shocked. I suspect it's the first time any student has ever answered him back.

"I said I won't come to see you – not after class, or any time. You're not my tutor any more."

"How dare you? Do you want to gain a law degree?"

All the stress from the last few weeks accumulates like thunderclouds gathering for a storm. The air around the lecture theatre crackles with electricity, and then the storm breaks.

"Do you know what? I don't actually care. I don't want to get a law degree at the expense of my self-esteem. I don't want to get a law degree if I have to sell my body in order to stay on the course, and I don't want to get a law degree if I ever have to see you again."

I grab my bag and stomp down the stairs to the nearest exit. As I open the door, the silence in the theatre changes to a loud cheer and some applause.

I smile and leave, allowing the door to close behind me, even as I hear Leeson trying to regain control of the class.

I head out of the building and go to the Students' Union. I sit in the bar with a diet coke. It's still only ten-fifteen – too early for cider, whatever the circumstances. The bar is almost empty; just me and the barman – a student from a less demanding course than mine, I expect. He's busy cleaning glasses, so I leave him to it, and focus on what's just happened.

I've quit my degree. That's all Dad's hopes gone up in smoke. He'll be livid. What made me do it?

Such a culmination of events: Rick's death – life's too short to waste it doing something I hate. Obviously Leeson's behaviour, topped with Vince's, Greg's and those lads that attacked me – just because I'm female, I shouldn't have to submit to abuse. I want to make a difference. I want to join the police force. Stuff my degree. If I'm earning a living in the police, Dad won't need to support me any more. I feel bad about Ian – he's going to bear the brunt of it, but I know he'd support my decision.

I finish my drink and catch the bus back to Halls. Before I contact Wendy Lucas, I need to solve the Rick mystery. It's been far too long since I worked on it, and now I have to prove that I've got what it takes to make it in the police force.

Back in Halls, I retrieve my phone money, and try again to call Dan. Alan answers.

"Hello, Alan here."

"Hi, is Dan there please? It's Becky."

"He's popped out." The phone goes dead.

What is going on? Doesn't Dan want to speak to me? Or does Alan not want Dan to speak to me? Very strange. I know Dan's been depressed and upset about Rick. Maybe if I sort out what happened, then that's one thing I can do to help.

I return to my room and find the box that contains the

photos I took of Rick's letters before I gave them to Wendy. There are also photos of his room. I'm pleased I took those. There's no way I'll be going back in there, not with Vince occupying it now.

I look through them, searching for clues. Nothing obvious appears, but it's useful to remind myself what I found: the powder shapes, the foil with the crumbs, and the note. Obviously the one piece of evidence I didn't get to see was the body. I shiver. In some ways I'm pleased about that. No detective ever wants to come across the body of a friend.

I grab my room key, and go along to Martin's room. I knock on the door, and wait. There's no answer, and I'm preparing to return to my room, when he comes along the corridor.

"Becky, are you alright?"

"Yes, fine thanks," I start guiltily. "Except that I've quit my course. I guess we need to discuss what happens next, but that's not why I'm here."

"Come along to the common room – it's likely to be empty now."

"Thanks."

"So why are you here? We'll discuss the other matter shortly."

"Did you attend the inquest for Rick?"

"I had to attend, yes. It was much sooner that I would have expected."

"Did they say how long he'd been dead before he was found?"

"They said it was probably less than an hour. The body was still warm – or at least as warm as would be expected in January, although the heating in these Halls is quite adequate."

"So, if he'd killed himself, it must have been in response to something that had happened early that morning, rather than the previous night." I look anxiously at Martin. It would be great to prove that at least Dan didn't have anything to do with it.

"Well, perhaps, but it could have been that he'd had time

to think about things by then."

"Do you think Rick was the type to do something like that in cold blood?" I hesitate. "You know you asked me to pack up all his things? His clothes were a strange contradiction – so flamboyant on the outside, but conventional and neat on the inside."

"He was a nice young man, but a complex one. I assumed he had some depressive issues, but I didn't know him that well."

"What made you think he was depressed?"

"Well, I suppose I didn't think of it at all until he was found dead."

"So there might have been no reason for him to kill himself? Which leaves murder."

"As I said to you the other day, stirring things up could cause more trouble than it saves."

"Not if we find the real killer, with the motive and everything." I stand up. "Thanks so much. You've been a great help."

Back at my room, I count out all my 10p pieces, emptying a few from my purse too. The photos are still strewn across my desk. I gather them up and put all except one back in the box. I take this one, along with the coins, down to the phone box in the courtyard. There are some calls that shouldn't be overheard.

Chapter Thirty-Two
Tuesday 21/2/89

Daniel

I don't know what day it is. I've been fed seven times – tinned soup and increasingly stale rolls, plus water (a plastic bottle with every meal) – and the bucket has been replaced with a clean one three times now. I've had nothing to do except sleep and think. Sleep is infinitely preferable, but it doesn't always happen when I most need it.

My sight has been gradually getting better though. Each time Alan visits, I can see him a bit more clearly. Perhaps in more ways than just visually, because although he's not expanded on his previous comments, he has reiterated them. I still don't really understand why I'm here, or what Dad did wrong. Dad can be a ruthless bastard, so it doesn't totally surprise me that he's caused serious offence, but I still don't know why Alan's taking it out on me.

I've been lying awake for a few hours when the door opens again. My vision is definitely okay now, as I see immediately that it's not Alan who's appeared with food and water.

"Rachel! Have you come to rescue me?"

"I wish I could, Dan. I know this isn't your fault. How's your head?"

A heavy lump settles in my stomach. I'd always thought Rachel would rescue me.

"My head's okay. I can see now. I wish someone would tell me why I'm here though."

"It's not my story. But I'll ask Alan to fill you in when he's down here later."

"Why am I here?"

"I can't tell you that. But I want to warn you that this cellar is very well insulated, so when people come round they can't hear you. Not that you've made any noise. You've been very good."

"Did you expect me to make a noise? I'm completely at your mercy. Why would I risk my life to shout for help? I always suspected no one would hear me anyway."

"I really am sorry, Daniel. You're a nice lad. We've caused you so much pain, one way or another."

"How do you mean?"

"Another secret – again, not for me to tell. I just wanted you to know that none of it was my idea." She flushes, and hesitates as though she's about to say something else, but then she opens the bag she's carrying, and extracts a full pie dish and a flask. "It's cold down here. I figured you could use something a bit more substantial than thin soup and last week's rolls."

She hands me the pie and a fork and spoon.

"Thanks. That smells good." My mouth is watering. I break the pie crust with the spoon, and take a mouthful – meat, potato and peas. "Wow. That's lovely. Thanks, Rachel." She might not be rescuing me, but by the time I've finished the pie, I'm full for the first time since I got down here.

"I made it. I'm pleased you like it." Her smile is warm and perhaps a bit shy. I'm reminded of the sweet girl I was drawn to when we first met, and I don't understand how she got involved with Alan. She must be really besotted to assist him with this. But then, he was charming and kind when I first met him, so maybe it's time I grew up and realised that not everyone is as they seem.

She watches me as I wipe my mouth on the napkin she brought me. A napkin – this is definite luxury.

"I'll leave you with the flask. It's tea with soya milk. Alan won't allow normal milk with meat, and neither would I. Drink it at your leisure. Alan will be back later." Her voice is strange, as though she knows things she's not happy about. But I already know that's true, so why am I suddenly afraid.

"Don't go, Rachel, please. I feel safer when you're here." It's not entirely true, but I'm desperate for some company.

"Sorry, Dan. I've got to get to work. I'll see you again soon though. Take care."

She's gone. The door's locked behind her. I pour myself a cup of tea from the flask. The lid is a cup with a thin plastic handle. I can see it clearly. I have a few mouthfuls of tea before I suddenly realise that Rachel left me with something else. There's a small lantern near the door. I stand up, and stagger over to get the light. I'm not sure why I'm staggering, but I haven't moved much in the last few days. No wonder my legs are wobbly.

With the lantern at my side, I sit back down on my blankets, and survey the room. It's still dingy, even with the dim light. I feel strangely woozy. I manage to fumble for the switch on the lantern. If I'm going to have a sleep, I don't want to waste the battery. The wooziness gets worse, and then swallows me up.

When I come round, my head is pounding, and nausea is building in my stomach. I try to summon the strength to go to the bucket. I don't want to throw up on my blankets.

But there's been a change. My arms are no longer free. They're tied behind my back, wrenching my shoulders into painful positions. My ankles are also restrained. I'm clearly going nowhere just yet. I take some deep breaths to stem the nausea. It works, but only just. Bile fills my mouth before I can force it back down. The taste is disgusting. I need another sip of that tea. The lantern is either still off or has been taken away. I don't know which.

My mind is clearing though. There must have been something in the tea or in that pie. The secret ingredient that knocked me out so they could come in and tie me up.

Tears fill my eyes. Bitter, angry tears. I can't believe they both betrayed me so badly. They were supposed to bring me to God. Isn't that what Kabbalah is about? But then this was never a real Kabbalah group. I've been taken in. Was it just set up to fool me? What about all those other people who came along for Friday night dinners? Were they taken in too, or are they all Alan's friends – willing to do anything to help him out? Worse still, do they all have a grudge against Dad?

The tears fall. I'm lying on my side, on the blanket, with my head on an increasingly damp pillow.

I try to wriggle my hands, hoping to free them, or at least loosen the bonds. How am I supposed to get to the bucket now? The binding seems to tighten the more I wriggle. How does that work? I give up and lie still, waiting with rising impatience for Alan to appear.

Chapter Thirty-Three
Wednesday 22/2/89

Becky

I catch the bus into Manchester to meet Joanna at Victoria Station at one-fifteen as arranged. There was a letter from her in the post this morning. It confirmed the time for meeting, even though we'd discussed it on the phone on Monday. But the most important thing was the photo. I study it on the bus. The photo shows a girl with long black straight hair, with rings through her eyebrow, nose, and – from what I could see of her ears – several in each ear. The girl in the photo looks terrifying, but she sounded friendly on the phone.

As I get off the bus and start to walk to the railway station, butterflies are going in my stomach. Am I doing the right thing? Will Joanna be able to help me?

The train is due in three minutes. I wait on the concourse. The butterflies are flapping vigorously, and I feel a bit queasy. I watch as the train pulls in, and the doors open, releasing a hundred or so people on to the wet platform. It's only when the crowds thin as they emerge onto the main concourse that I see her. Only the black hair alerts me – as the jewellery is all gone, and the hair is tied back in a long plait. She looks about twelve.

"Hi, are you Becky?" Her accent is Scottish, but not broad.

"Yes. Hi, Joanna."

She grins. "Sorry for the photo, pet. Couldn't resist. That was me a couple of months ago, when it all kicked off. Well – you read the letters. You know Dad died, and Ellen wanted the house. It's amazing what effect you can have with a change of style. At first I thought I was going to have to go for the tattoos, but she eventually decided all the rings were too much: the nose-ring, eyebrow ring, earrings, and the swearing." She laughs, a bubbling, pretty sound. "I changed my laugh too, specially for her. Do you want to hear it?"

I nod, a bit bemused – it's not often that I can't get a word in.

The resultant bellow is raucous and grating. I put my hands over my ears.

"Aye, exactly. I practised in my room for days. The bitch thought I was laughing at my dad's passing, but focussing on getting rid of her was all that kept me sane." She pauses for half a second and looks around the station. "Can we get some lunch? I'm starving."

I guide her to the nearest Spud-U-Like, and we sit on the plastic chairs and eat baked spuds with tuna, while she entertains me with tales of her journey. When she finally pauses to take a mouthful of potato, I grab the opportunity to interject.

"Thanks for coming down. I really appreciate it. It's been tough, and there's been lots going on that I kind of need some help with."

"Why would you choose me? We've spoken once. We never met before today. Surely you'd choose someone you know well and trust?"

"You knew Rick. I need to find out why he died. I'm sorry if it's mean bringing you down here when you were friends with him."

"Aye, kind of friends. We laughed a lot, talked a lot, and flirted a lot. There was never anything in it though. The letters were just a laugh. And it's not mean. Rick would never, ever have killed himself. I want to find out which bastard killed him. I'd bloody hang the sod myself!"

"Why do you say Rick wouldn't have killed himself? I didn't think he did, but I had nothing but a gut feeling to support that."

"When he and I met, he'd just lost his Uncle Ben to suicide. Ben had left a note. He was a gambler, and had run into massive debt. He couldn't handle it. Rick was gutted –

he'd been very close with his uncle, and felt guilty, like he should have been able to help. Rick had a year out before Uni, so I guess he'd have been a year older than you. I'm a year older again. We met on holiday, just after Ben died. His parents hadn't wanted to cancel as it was the last family holiday, but Rick said the atmosphere was dreadful. He couldn't stand it, so he'd meet up with me and we'd go for long walks and chat a lot." She pauses briefly, and smiles a dreamy smile. "We'd snog a bit too. We were mostly just friends though. Anyway, he was furious that no one had been able to help Ben, and even angrier that his dad had allowed them to come on holiday the day after the funeral. Ben was his dad's brother."

"I can imagine. Poor Rick."

"Aye, it was a hard time for him. But the important thing is that he ranted for ages about how awful suicide is for the family. He wouldn't dream of doing that himself."

"Oh God, so his mum and dad must be thinking that Rick has followed in his uncle's footsteps. We have to find Rick's killer so they don't have to carry that around with them too."

"You said on the phone that your best pal has been struggling with it too. Was she in love with Rick? So many people were. I wasn't, but I really liked him and fancied him a bit too. He had so much charisma, it was hard not to."

"Dan is a boy, not a girl, but yes, I think he was in love with Rick."

"Oh shit!"

"Why do you say that?"

"According to Ben's suicide note, the thing that tipped him over the edge was discovering he had AIDS. Rick definitely wasn't in the mood to deal with gays afterwards. If your pal told Rick that he was gay, Rick would have freaked out."

"That happened the night before Rick died. Dan opened up to him, and Rick apparently did freak out then. The next morning, Dan tried to knock on Rick's door – I don't know if he wanted to apologise or just to ask if they could still be friends. When they got the door open – Dan had to get all sorts of people involved to do that – Rick was there, dead." I shiver.

"Show me your Halls. Am I okay to sleep on your floor for a couple of days?"

"Yeah, sure. The house tutor likes me, so I'll be able to get around him if anyone says anything. Other people have visitors anyway. It should be fine." We've finished eating now, so I pick up her holdall, as it looks lighter than the huge rucksack she has with her. "Blimey, what have you got in here? It weighs a ton."

"I'll take it. I'm used to carrying all my stuff around. I just have a lot of gear. I'll show you when we get back."

We head back to the bus station with me carrying nothing, and Joanna with that huge rucksack on her back and carrying the holdall in her left hand. I glance at her. She's a couple of inches shorter than me, maybe five foot two or three, but she's really slim. Her gear must weigh nearly as much as she does.

Back in my room, we decide on a plan of campaign. We head to the common room first. It's empty except for Greg and Vince. I take a deep breath. I've not had a chance to tell Joanna about these two.

"Hey Becks, is your friend as much of a slut as you are?" Greg's crass remark sets my teeth on edge, and I'm about to make a rude reply when Joanna turns to me.

"Leave this to me," she mutters.

Next thing I know, Greg is on the ground, howling in agony, as she gives him a kick in the balls.

Vince looks at Greg, then at Joanna, then at me. "Fuck. I'm going." His face turns a shade of green as Greg's yells get louder, and then he scarpers.

Joanna stops kicking and glares at him.

"If I ever hear you've been offensive again, I'll tie you in so many friggin' knots, you'll not be able to stretch out for a month. Keep your sodding mouth shut, and show some respect."

We leave the common room.

"I forgot to tell you about them. Vince, the guy who ran, now occupies Rick's old room. Greg is a prick." I feel myself go red – I don't really want to go into details.

"Aye, I can tell. No bother – he won't hassle you again. I'm going to teach you some moves." She grins, a mischievous grin that makes me like her even more. I think we're going to become very good friends.

We leave the common room and head down Dan's corridor. There's no point knocking on his door, so we start with Nathan. He's not in his room, and I know that Peter (the occupant of the room next door) practically lives with his girlfriend, and has done since November. He pops back every couple of weeks for a bit of space, but he wasn't in Halls the day Rick died, so there's no point in bothering with him.

Next to Peter's room is Sanjay. I knock on his door.

The door latch clicks, and I glance at Joanna. She looks calm, but there's a muscle twitching in her cheek, so perhaps she's as nervous as I am.

"Hi Becks. Is everything okay?"

"Hi Sanjay, this is Joanna. She's helping me investigate Rick's death, as she's an old friend of his." We'd rehearsed the patter beforehand, and decided to be as open as possible.

"Do you want to come in? It's not too messy at the moment." He waves us inside, and I glance round with interest. In tidiness, it's somewhere between mine and Dan's, but that leaves a pretty big range. There are no clothes on the floor; they all seem to occupy a half-full laundry basket in the corner. Books and tapes are arranged in piles on the floor, but there's space to walk, and Sanjay sits on the bed, leaving me and Joanna to sit in the chairs.

"Thanks for inviting us in, Sanjay. As Becky said, I was friends with Rick, and I know there's no way he'd have killed himself. So we're looking for a killer, and it's hard to know where to start, so we're enlisting your help." She grins. "You seem an observant kind of guy, so I wanted to ask: did you see anyone strange hanging around on the day he died?"

"That's so weird that you've asked, and particularly now, as I hadn't registered it before."

"What do you mean?" My stomach turns over – surely we

can't have struck lucky this early in our investigations.

"A week and a half ago, a woman came to collect Dan. I saw her in the lift with him. I recognised her, but I hadn't given it any thought before, not consciously. I wasn't sure where I knew her from anyway."

"What's a woman from a week and a half ago got to do with Rick?" My brain is struggling to fit things together. "Slow down and explain. I'm getting confused."

"She was in the tenth floor foyer the day Rick died. I saw her on my way back from breakfast. I'd got up early to do an essay."

"You were in pyjamas when I got to the common room," I interrupt, confused.

"Yeah, well after breakfast, I felt a bit sick, so decided to go back to bed, and leave the essay for an hour or so. That's beside the point though. That woman was there. She was a stranger, and she was wearing black gloves. Then we found out Rick was dead, and I kind of forgot about her."

I can't help being sceptical at this. I like Sanjay, but he's not thick. How could he not be suspicious?

He seems to notice my expression. "Sorry, Becks. Apart from the gloves – and to be fair it was pretty damn cold that day – she just looked like a nice normal woman who'd either been visiting or found herself on the wrong floor or something. Honestly, there was nothing about her to suggest she might have killed someone."

"Okay, so the woman who was here the day Rick died turned up again, a week and a half ago, to pick up Dan. What made you realise it was the same person?"

"It was Vince. He kept going on about 'Dan's pimp', and this morning he was laughing about it with Greg – they were going on and on about it. It suddenly clicked where I'd seen her before."

I turn to Joanna. "I think we need to tell the police. I'm friendly with the Sergeant on the case. Wendy's really kind. Do you want to come with me? Then we need to find Dan. I can't believe he's safe if this woman was Rick's killer."

"Aye, I'm sure you're right. Thanks, Sanjay, you've been a

great help. We'll tell Becky's Sergeant everything. She might come to interview you, but I'm sure that will be fine."

Before heading to the police station, I ask Martin to let me into Dan's room, confiding that I'm really worried as Dan should have been back on Sunday.

"Dan said he'd leave the address in his room in case anything happened. Not that either of us thought it would, but he knew I was worried about him generally. I just need to find his address book."

"Alright, but I need to come in with you. I can't allow students to go searching each other's rooms without supervision."

Chapter Thirty-Four
Wednesday 22/2/89

Daniel

Alan turned up briefly last night. Just long enough to give some soup through a straw, and bring the bucket near enough for me to wee into. He wouldn't untie me, but helped me to stand up and pulled down my jeans and pants so I could do what I had to. He refused to speak to me the whole time except for brief instructions.

When he left me (still standing), I was angry and exhausted, but eventually managed to lie down without hurting myself too much, and fell into an uncomfortable doze.

I wake up desperate for another wee. It's pitch black in here now, but Alan used the lantern last night, and I could see that he left the bucket in the nearest corner when he left. The problem is that I'm completely disorientated after lying down, so I don't know which way that corner is from here. I wriggle into a position where I can propel myself along the floor, with bent knees, and shuffle on my shoulder, hip and knee. It hurts everywhere, particularly those bits in contact with the floor, like my upper arm and hip, but I keep going, until I bump my head gently on the wall. It's a good start. I do some difficult visualisation in my head, and praying I've got it right, turn slightly to move along the wall. It takes a few minutes to get to the corner, but no bucket. Shit. I really am disorientated. With a complicated manoeuvre, I turn myself round a hundred and eighty degrees, and start to shuffle along in the other direction. I've lost track of time when I eventually reach the bucket, not that I had much of a concept of what time it is anyway.

I suddenly realise that although I've found the bucket, I have no way of getting myself upright. Tears sting the back of my eyelids, but I don't want to give in. I wriggle my hands into a position where I can use the wall to help me sit up, and then to stand. It seems to take forever, and now I have the task of pulling down jeans and pants. A lot more wriggling, and it's done.

A moment later, with a now empty bladder, I'm about to start pulling everything back into place – as much as possible with my hands tied behind my back – when the door opens. I'm marginally relieved to see it's Alan rather than Rachel, but with the light from the lantern, I must look pretty pathetic. The relief is quickly replaced by fear.

"For goodness sake, Dan. Couldn't you have waited?"

"Obviously not. It was enough of a challenge getting to the bloody bucket in the first place. Why am I tied up?"

"I can't have you escaping. Until your dear father turns up to rescue you, you'll stay as you are. Except that you don't seem able to cope with clothes. I think you'll find it a lot easier without." He pulls my trousers and pants down as he speaks. "Can't get them over the ropes. Shame. I'll have to do this." He extracts a huge pair of scissors from a bag slung round his neck, and proceeds to cut through my clothes.

"Hey, you can't do that. What if Rachel walks in?" It's a stupid defence, but it's the first thing to come to mind.

"She won't. I'll make sure she doesn't visit you again. She only came that time to give you the drugged food. We reckoned you wouldn't trust me any more."

I try to move away from those giant shears, but with my ankles tied together, and Alan attacking my clothes, I fall backwards, against the wall. The momentum is too strong for my hands to stop me falling, and I end up on the floor. Alan finishes his job and my jeans lie in frayed pieces around me.

"You look a bit stupid now. I might as well finish the job."

"What job?"

"Apparently it's a power thing, but depriving hostages of clothes makes them more docile. Stay still, or I'll end up cutting you, and I'm not ready to do that just yet."

As he deprives me of my sweatshirt and t-shirt – both now fit for nothing but the bin – I try to get my head around what's happening and to overcome the feeling of degradation. Despite the cold, my face is warm with embarrassment.

"Why are you doing this?"

"I don't suppose I've explained yet, have I?" Alan puts the tatters in his bag, and leans against the wall near the door. He's staring at me, and I shuffle round to the side so I'm shielding certain bits from view with my legs. He shakes his head. "You can do that if it makes you feel better. Anyway, I've got a story to tell, so you might as well make yourself as comfortable as you can."

I stare at him in disbelief. I'm tied up, he's taken my clothes, and it's bloody freezing, and he's talking about comfortable!

"About five years ago, my twin brother, Elliot, worked for your dad. Elliot had just finished his accountancy exams and was excited about getting a job in a large corporation. The fact that it was based near home was even better."

"You lived in Birmingham? You don't have the accent."

"Yes, not so far from you, although we didn't move in the same circles. I lived in London until I was fifteen. Anyway, Elliot worked hard, but then his fiancée was killed in a car crash. Then he began to struggle. And your father sacked him."

"I'm not my dad. I wouldn't have behaved like that, so why are you doing this to me?"

"So he can watch someone he loves suffer. I want him to watch and understand as you get physically and mentally weaker. When I've finished with you, you'll be begging me to kill you, because your life will be as unbearable as Elliot's was."

I shiver, this time not from the cold. Alan doesn't understand me though. He thinks I've got further to go in the realms of unbearable, but nothing he can do to me comes close to losing Rick. I've already hit the bottom – I got as far as the bridge before something pulled me back. Despite everything, my will to live is stronger than my pain. Whatever degradation and horror Alan throws at me, he can't compete.

I don't answer him. He doesn't deserve a response.

"Elliot killed himself in the end. And so will you."

I turn my head away from him. The door is open a crack, and Rachel's voice reaches me. "Alan, are you down there? Will you be long?"

"No, love, I'm just on my way." He looks at me, hatred showing now in his eyes. Even in the dim light of the lantern I can see it. "I might come back later to feed you. It depends." He pulls the door to, but doesn't close it properly, so I can still hear their voices.

"What's in there?" asks Rachel.

"Dan's clothes."

"Was that really necessary?"

"Yeah, I think it was. He was giving me some lip. He needs to know who's in charge around here. Anyway, I've told him about Elliot. Even so, he'll never understand how much I loved my brother. He was my twin. Losing him was like losing a limb. Worse even. I have to do this, Rache. After what you did to reel him in, we can't back out now."

"You'd better close that door properly." Rachel's comment kills any last hope of escape.

I try to digest all the new information. I don't understand the full details, but basically, Alan and Rachel enticed me here so he could get revenge on my dad for his twin's suicide. I'm screwed. Dad is a ruthless bastard, and won't care enough to rescue me. I can only pray that Sharon will persuade him, or that Becky will find me.

Becky, please find me. I need you.

Chapter Thirty-Five
Thursday 23/2/89

Becky

Heavy snow yesterday caused us to postpone our trip to the police station. I tried phoning the police – I badly wanted to tell Wendy of the latest development – but the lines were down. After trying several of the phone boxes in the courtyard, we apprehensively shelved our plans and got some food from the dining room.

Joanna spent the night in a sleeping bag on my floor, and we're now breakfasted and preparing to go to see Wendy.

"Becky, I'm going to take my stuff and go back to the railway station after we've seen your police detective. I need to get back home today. Even though I've evicted the old cow and changed the locks, if I spend more than a night away from home, she'll be back and find her way in."

After several hours of chat, I know more about Joanna's stepmother than I could have ever imagined, so that doesn't surprise me. She sounds like an evil witch.

"Okay, have you got everything?" I'm impatient to get away. The snow has cleared, but the sky's grey and heavy-looking. A knock on the door startles me, as I was about to open it anyway.

"Call for you, Becky." It's one of the girls on my corridor. I thank her and leave Joanna to sort herself out while I go and answer the phone.

"Hello, Becky here, who is it?"

"Oh Becky, please help, it's Sharon Ledermann."

"Sharon, hi, what's the matter?"

"Dad had a letter this morning. From a guy called Alan.

He's got Dan and he's holding him hostage until Dad sends an insane amount of money and an apology."

I sink down onto the chair next to the phone, as my legs wobble. My mind goes blank for a minute, overwhelmed by this information.

"Becky, are you still there?"

"Yeah, sorry. It's a bit much to take in."

"We're still trying to get our heads around it here too. The letter arrived about an hour ago, but Dad's been dithering and protesting that he can't get his hands on that amount of money." Sharon lowers her voice. "I'm scared. I don't know if Dad cares enough about Dan to save him. I know that's an awful thing to say, but this guy Alan wants a million pounds."

"How long has he given you to get the money to him?"

"He says we've got to take it to a safety deposit box in Birmingham at two o'clock this afternoon. It's crazy. We'll never manage to get the money in time."

"That might give me a window of time to rescue Dan though. I reckon Alan will want his money as soon as possible, so probably he'll be in Birmingham by two-thirty at the latest. That gives me from about one until four to get Dan out."

"How are you going to do that?"

"I'm going to the police to get some help."

"Becky, the letter says 'No police'." Sharon's voice is desperate.

I totally get it. Inside I'm panicking, but I need to stay calm and focus on action now. It sounds melodramatic, but Dan's life might just depend on me.

"Try not to worry. I'll be really discreet about the police, and to be honest, I was going to see them today about something else anyway. Also, it was the letter to you that gave that instruction. If he's got anyone watching, they'll be watching at your end, not here. My visit to the police won't even be noticed. I promise. Give me your number. As soon as I hear anything, I'll let you know."

"Okay. Meanwhile, I'll try to persuade Dad. Maybe if we

can get some of the money together, it will help Dan somehow."

We say our goodbyes, and with a heart full of fear I return to my room to find Joanna ready and waiting to go. I shut the door behind me and sit on the bed.

"You look as if you're going to faint. Put your head between your knees." She holds my head down until I feel as though all the blood is pooling in my brain. I wave my hand around and she lets me up. "Is that better, pet? You still don't look great. What happened?"

"Dan's being held hostage. That was his sister on the phone. They've had a ransom demand, and Alan also wants an apology, and, bloody hell, I forgot to ask what for."

"So, are we still going to see Wendy? Or do we go straight for the rescue?"

I explain about the ransom drop, and why we should attempt the rescue at about half past two. I still feel a bit shaky, but it's time to get a grip on myself.

"Let's go to see Wendy then, and aim to be at Alan's house shortly after he's gone."

Arriving at the police station at eleven, I ask for Wendy Lucas.

"Is she expecting you?" asks the elderly man at the desk.

"No, but please could you tell her that Becky White is here, and it's urgent. Someone's in danger." I get a sceptical look in return, but he picks up the phone and makes a call.

"She'll be down to see you in a few minutes. Take a seat." He indicates the chairs against the wall, and we sit and wait.

"Becky?" Wendy is at reception. I didn't notice her come in as I was too busy plotting Dan's rescue. "Are you okay? Do you want to come through?"

"Thanks. This is Joanna."

"The Joanna from the letters?"

Wow, that was quick. I smile and nod.

"So pleased to meet you, Joanna. I'm DS Wendy Lucas – I've been working on Rick's case. Come through, then you can tell me all about it."

Half an hour later, and Wendy knows as much as we do. We didn't leave anything out, and finish up with telling her about Dan.

"I can't spare a lot of people to help you this afternoon. There's a drill going on in Central Manchester, but Daniel's clearly in danger. I'll swing it somehow." She turns to Joanna. "Do you have to leave this afternoon? I'd feel a lot happier if Becky had more help, but I'm only going to be able to manage a couple of officers. Oh, what the hell, the drill can happen without me. Someone can fill me in later. You girls are more important. I can't let you go in there alone."

"Thanks." I turn to Joanna. "Would you be able to stay a while longer?"

"If you really want me to stay, Becks, I suppose I could. I might need to get the police to evict the old witch if she comes back, but Dan's more important. I've not met him, but Rick mentioned him in one of his letters, and said he was lucky to have made such a great pal. I'll do this for Rick, and for you."

My throat clogs up, and I can't speak for a moment, so I just nod, and touch her briefly on the arm.

"Aye, okay. I'm staying. What's the plan, Wendy?"

Chapter Thirty-Six
Thursday 23/2/89

Daniel

It's freezing cold in here. Several parts of my body have gone numb, and my ability to think has become severely impaired. I haven't slept properly since Alan left, taking my clothes, my dignity, and any hope of being released.

I tried rolling around the floor to keep warm, but the cold concrete is unforgiving, and it kills my shoulders, as my arms are still tied behind my back. I eventually settled into an uneasy doze, but since I woke properly a few hours ago, I've had nothing to do except pray and panic. Alan's brought me no food today, and no reprieve from the pitch darkness, as there's no source of daylight to penetrate this room.

I'm drifting into despair when a strange, scraping sound comes to my ears. Unsure what or who it might be, I twist myself into a position where a tiny amount of privacy is preserved, and wait to see if it happens again. It's not the usual sound of the key in the lock, but seems to be originating from the same direction. There's another scrape and a click. The door opens, and a torch shines around the room.

"Hello?" My voice is scratchy from the cold. I feel like I'm coming down with the flu, but it doesn't matter at the moment. Someone's here.

"Dan? Are you okay?"

Becky! Thank God! She shines the torch around until it alights on me. She must realise the condition I've been left in, because the torch is lowered to the floor, and turned a little away from me. I can see her now in the dim light away from the main beam. She slides a rucksack from her back and takes off her coat, which she brings over and places over me.

"That will have to do for a moment. Let's get those ropes off you." Her voice is thick with emotion, but she's keeping it together really well.

I feel a fraction better with the coat over me.

Becky delves in the rucksack again, bringing out a number of items, including a sharp knife. She approaches me, and goes first to my feet, cutting firmly through the rope keeping my ankles together.

"Okay, Dan, I need to do your wrists now. I'm going behind you. Don't worry, I'll be really careful."

I feel her move the coat away, just enough to expose my wrists. She's part-way completed sawing through the rope, when there's a piercing whistle.

"Shit. That's Joanna warning us we've got company, and I need to finish this, and get you out of here." She speeds up and the knife catches my arm.

"Ow."

"Oh shit, I'm sorry, Dan. I'm trying to be quick. Nearly done."

"Okay." A second later, my arms are free, and I wrap the coat more securely around me. I sit up and feel light-headed, but this is not the time to be pathetic.

"How did this bloody door get open?" Alan sounds livid. The room becomes several shades lighter, as he comes in with the lantern. Becky is standing next to me, pointing the knife in Alan's direction.

"How did you get in?" He fires the question at Becky – as though it matters. She's here, and I'm no longer tied up, although I'm weaker than a new-born kitten.

"Never you mind. You're going to let us out, and forget all about this. Why aren't you picking up the ransom from Dan's dad?"

"How do you know about that?" He doesn't wait for an answer. "There was no ransom. I didn't expect one, to be honest. Rachel went to pick it up, and phoned me about five minutes ago to say the bag was empty except for a hundred pounds and a note. I got back from shopping about a minute before she called."

Pain stabs in my chest. Is that all I'm worth to my dad? A measly hundred pounds?

"What did the note say?" Becky seems to be stalling for time, but I'm curious too, somewhere in amongst the hurt.

"I can't remember the exact words. I'm not a machine. It was something like, '*It's not my fault your brother killed himself. He was an incompetent idiot, who allowed his personal life to interfere with my business. Release my son, or I'll sue your brother's estate for damages to my company. The hundred pounds is to cover your expenses, and is against my better judgement*'. Your father's insane. I've been planning this ever since Elliot died. I found out where you were going to Uni, by contacting your school. As soon as they said you'd be coming to Manchester, I got myself a house, and started to build a following. Then I sought you out at the J-Soc ball. I was watching and waiting for my opportunity. I knew I had to get you here somehow."

"You're the one who's crackers," says Becky. "How on earth…? Oh! Oh my God, that's why Rachel killed Rick."

"What? Rachel killed Rick? How do you know?" The questions tumble out, but the pain in my chest increases. I liked Rachel. Even when I knew she was helping Alan keep me here, I thought she was basically a decent person. She betrayed me.

Becky looks at me, then cautiously over at Alan. She's still holding the knife firmly in her hands, and her grip appearing to be tighter than when he first came in to the cellar.

"Rachel was spotted by a lad in our house, both when she was picking up Dan for this visit, and the morning Rick was found dead. The previous day, Rick was sent a cake wrapped in tinfoil. There was a note, signed with a squiggle, suggesting he should have it as a late-night treat. The crumbs were analysed by the police, and contained sleeping pills. They also found a lethal dose of barbiturates in his body, injected into him that morning when he was drugged and docile. But it seems a bit far-fetched to kill Rick just to get

Dan to join your group."

"That bit was Rachel's idea. I'd sent her along in December before the end of term to get to know Rick, so we could find out how best to get to Dan. Then at the beginning of this term, she said we should kill Rick to get Dan into a state. It seemed a bit far-fetched to me too, but Rache was adamant it would work. How did you find out all this anyway?"

"I took photos of everything in Rick's room before it was cleared out, and one of the photos was of a box with stamps on. The box was big enough to contain a cake, and was postmarked Salford. That ties in with the location of this house, which is on the edge of Broughton Park. There were other things too."

"Circumstantial." Alan is sweating though. There's a slight scuffing noise outside the door, but his attention is on Becky, and I don't want to draw attention to it in case it's someone else on my side. If not, then I'm a bit more alert anyway.

"You've got motive. You needed to destroy one of Dan's friends – someone he cared enough about to drive him to seek solace. You then made sure you were there to provide that solace, until he was comfortable enough to stay with you alone. You used Rachel to do all your dirty work – killing Rick, befriending Dan, picking him up, going to Birmingham to get the ransom. What do you have on her? Or is she stupid enough to do have done it all for love?"

"She did it for love, yeah. I needed an assistant. Rachel and I were attracted to each other when I first moved here. She quickly became obsessed with me, and was ready to do anything I asked her. She went a bit weird when I got her to befriend Rick though, and I had to go along with some stuff to keep her on my side."

My mouth drops open. I can't believe she was in on it all the time, and that she killed Rick.

I find my voice. "Why Rick?"

"We were watching you for a long time, observing your comings and goings. You were with him more than anyone else, and had these big puppy-dog eyes whenever you looked at him. It was pretty obvious to me how you felt. So it was just a matter of setting it up. Then the next day, you were wandering the snowy streets in despair, just waiting for me to pick you up and make everything better."

"Why did you make it all about Kabbalah?" asks Becky. I hadn't got that far yet; my brain is still catching up with the fact that they killed Rick to get at me.

"Kabbalah was in the news a lot when Elliot passed away. I looked into it at first as a way for coping. But then I turned things around in my head, and decided that a Kabbalistic group was the perfect way to get retribution." He moves suddenly, twisting Becky's arm behind her back, and grabbing the knife from her. It happens too fast, and we're now at a complete disadvantage.

"So, you don't honestly think I can let you out of here alive after all these revelations, do you?" he says. The knife is now pointing at Becky's throat. The scuffling sound comes again, very faintly. I pray for help.

Becky looks panicked for a moment, then there's a second of concentration, followed by a complicated manoeuvre. I don't know how, but she's got Alan on the floor, with the knife at his throat.

"Joanna? Wendy?" she calls out.

Who the hell are Joanna and Wendy?

A tall girl with dark hair strides into the room. She's carrying more rope, and between her and Becks they manage to get Alan trussed up in much the same way I was, but dressed.

"Hi Dan, I'm Joanna," she says in a soft Scottish accent. "I heard about you from Rick. He thought very highly of you."

My insides seem to dissolve, and suddenly tears are falling from my eyes. I try to blink them back, and a siren in the immediate vicinity helps. Distraction therapy. Alan's yells also help to keep the tears at bay. We need to get to safety before Rachel arrives.

The siren stops, and a minute or two later we're joined by several police officers – mostly male, but with one female amongst them. One of the men crouches down beside Alan, and reads him his rights. He's wanted for kidnapping, fraud and being an accomplice to murder. His legs are untied, and he's taken outside.

"Well done, girls. You've done a great job." The female officer turns to me. "Daniel? I'm Wendy Lucas, a police Sergeant and a friend of Becky's. One of my officers will get you some clothes, and we'll get you back to Halls, where you can relax. You're lucky to have such good friends. Becky's risked her life for you today."

Maybe I am lucky. Whilst I'm overwhelmed with anger that Rachel and Alan killed Rick to get to me, in some ways it's a relief that he didn't kill himself. I didn't drive him to that. I don't think I'll ever get over his death, but perhaps one day I'll find someone to love who loves me back.

I hope Becky does too. She deserves it.

Chapter Thirty-Seven
Friday 24/2/89

Becky

I slept late this morning, as we were at the police station until gone ten last night, while statements were taken, and Dan was examined and photographed. Joanna got the night train back to Edinburgh.

I've breakfasted now, and am waiting for Wendy. She promised me she'd visit this morning, to check up on Dan and update us on a few things.

There's a knock on the door, and I check myself in the mirror before answering. A pale face with dark-rimmed eyes stares back at me. I take a deep breath and open the door.

"You took your time, Becks. Did you not want to see me?" Dan holds out his arms, and I accept the silent offer of a hug.

"Of course I do. I didn't think you'd be up. They nearly sent you to hospital yesterday. You were bordering on having hypothermia." My voice is muffled against his shoulder. It terrifies me how lucky we were to find him in time. It could have all gone so badly.

"I need to find some normality, whatever that looks like." He steps away. "Are you going to invite me in?"

"You don't normally need inviting." I hold the door open for him, and we both sit on the bed, a little way apart, but facing each other. "Have you spoken to your dad and sister?"

"Just to Sharon. It was last night actually, from the police station. She was crying, but happy tears. She's jumping on the train tomorrow, and coming up to see me. Her teachers threw a strop for her missing school yesterday, but the letter arrived before she left. Just as well as it turned out. Anyway, she didn't dare ask for another day off – not now they know I'm okay."

"Is your dad not coming up?" I hardly dare ask, and hold my breath as Dan winces and looks away.

"I don't know. Sharon said he was subdued. Apparently he was angry that his actions were being used against me, but had no remorse for the consequences of his actions against Elliot." He stops and gazes out of the window for a moment, then turns to look back at me. "He also mentioned that I deserved to be punished for not giving up my nonsense."

"What?"

"He reckons this is my punishment for being gay."

"What did Sharon say?"

"She's mortified, but I made her tell me the truth." Dan looks down at the bed.

"What are you going to do? Will you go home at the end of term?"

"I have to. But as soon as I finish my degree, I'm going to get a job and move out. Maybe go to London. What about you? You said last night that you'd dropped out of your course." In between all the waiting around at the station, I'd given Dan a condensed version of events over the previous week and a half. Insane to think so much happened in that time, but then, it's only a month since Rick was killed, and it feels like a year.

"I don't know. Dad hasn't answered my letter yet. I don't know what I'm going to do, but I need to either find another course or get a job."

There's another rap on the door. I get up and open it, to find Wendy outside.

"Hi, come in. Dan's here."

"Good. I came to see both of you." She sits in the desk chair, and pulls it round to face us. "Daniel, how are you feeling today?"

"I'm a bit sore. I guess my muscles are protesting at having been tied up, but I've finally warmed up, and feel okay."

"Good. You do realise it will take you longer to get over

the mental scars, don't you?"

"Yeah. I slept for about two hours last night, then woke up in a sweat. It was a struggle to get up this morning. A panic attack forced me to seek out Becky."

"Why didn't you tell me?" Guilt overwhelms me that I didn't ask him how he's doing mentally.

"You gave me a hug. It helped. And then you were normal. Just asking me questions like you always do." He grins, and takes my hand in his. "You see, that's what you do, Becks. I don't need you to check up on me. Only to be around; to be here when I need you. I know I'm being selfish, but you're my best friend – probably my only friend now. Don't run out on me, okay?"

"Of course not." I squeeze his hand back. "I wouldn't run out on you. I'm not planning on leaving Manchester. I don't know what I'm going to do, but I like it here. I don't want to leave."

"There's an opening," Wendy says. "I wanted to speak to you about it today. Last night didn't seem to be the time or place. Before we come to that, though, I need to explain about Rachel, and why she decided that killing Rick would be a good idea."

"Oh my God, was it really Rachel's idea?" I ask.

"Yes. You know those letters between Rick and Joanna?"

"Yes."

"What letters?" Dan looks puzzled. I guess there's a lot that I've not told him yet.

"Rick had a... I don't want to upset you, Daniel, but Rick liked to write and receive dirty letters. It got him into trouble a few times. By a strange coincidence, there was a man in the cells yesterday – a domestic abuse case. It turned out his wife had got involved with Rick. This guy blackmailed Rick into stopping it, but he had a nasty temper. He clearly hasn't forgiven his wife."

"I hope she's okay." I turn to Dan. "Do you remember that guy in the pizza place? Do you reckon it was the same one?"

"Probably. How many more of these pen-pals did Rick have?" Dan asks Wendy.

"He had a friendship with Joanna that centred around the letters. They both had fun with it, and no harm was done. But when Rachel tried to befriend him, Rick seems to have decided that he could have a similar relationship with her. He sent her a number of letters. We arrested her yesterday, and I think she wanted to cooperate. Perhaps to reduce her sentence. Maybe she just wanted us to understand. Anyway, Daniel, she wrote you a letter."

Dan takes the letter, and peruses it for a moment. He takes some deep breaths, and then hands it to me.

"Read it out loud. I don't think I can take it in." His eyes are swimming, and his voice sounds choked.

I straighten the letter, and start to read aloud.

"Dear Dan,

"I'm so sorry we put you through so much. I'm genuinely relieved that you're now safe, but I need to tell you how it all came about.

"When I met Alan it was love at first sight. Sorry, I know it sounds clichéd, but as soon as I saw him, even before we spoke, I knew that he was the man for me, and I would do anything for him.

"It only took a few days before we started dating. It was last July, so we'd been together for five months before he told me his plans in December. He'd already told me about Elliot, so I knew he was hurt. I badly wanted to alleviate his pain, so when he asked me to get to know Rick, I quickly agreed.

"Rick and I became friendly, and I visited him in Edinburgh over the holidays. He thought I fancied him, and I had to put up with him kissing me. I wouldn't let it go any further though. But then he started sending me these letters. Fortunately he sent them to my dad's house. I never gave him Alan's address, and each of the letters was burned as soon as I got them. I know you and Rick were friends, so it hurts me to have to tell you this. He was a sick young man. The letters were obscene, suggesting acts I'd never even heard of. Whilst he was in Scotland, I could just destroy the letters, but I began to panic about what would happen when he returned

to Manchester. He'd already begun to say what he wanted us to do when he was back. He was very explicit about it. The letters made me want to vomit. It reached the point where I could barely read them. When one arrived I would skim through it, then throw it on the fire.

"The day before term began, Alan turned up seconds after the latest letter had gone up in flames. Panic ran through me. Although he'd sent me to befriend Rick, Alan would be livid if he knew what was happening now. You began to see what Alan could be capable of. Although I love him, I'd begun to be afraid of his anger.

"I suggested that killing Rick would be a way of speeding up the process of enticing you to join us. It was an appealing solution in so many ways. It sorted out my problems. It would enable me to do something for Alan to show him how far I would go for him. And it brought you to us.

"Alan agreed with my plan, and it was easy enough to carry out. I had the drugs already from a long history of sleeping problems. My GP had recently prescribed it in injectable form, and I already had the tablets in my cabinet. I collected the prescription, and sent the cake to Rick with a note. I knew he'd eat it. He loved chocolate cake. And I knew him well enough to know that he would save it for a late night treat. Easy enough for me to arrive early in the morning when he was docile and sleepy. He was pleased to see me, but not with-it enough to cause any problems. When I got him to sit on his chair, promising a massage, he complied without argument. So simple then to administer the injection. Bye bye Rick, and bye bye all those nasty letters.

"Again, I need to apologise to you, Dan, but he really wouldn't have been a good friend for you to have.

"Please don't tell Alan about the letters. Even now, I worry that he'll find out. If you tell him, I would just have to lie about it, but I wanted you to know the truth.

"Love Rachel."

I put the letter on the bed and glance at Dan. He's hiding his face in his hands, and his shoulders are shaking.

I rest my hand on his arm. "She sounds as though she's mentally ill. She was obsessed with Alan, for one thing. And to go to the extreme of murder on such a flimsy pretext – it's not normal."

"Becky's right, Daniel. We've only done an initial assessment so far, but it's more than likely that Rachel will end up in a psychiatric unit rather than a prison. But Alan will go to prison for what he's done to you, and for his involvement in Rick's murder."

"Good." Dan lifts his head from his hands. His face is pale except for the red rims around his eyes. I take his hand and squeeze it.

"What about that opening you mentioned?" Changing the subject seems to be the best way forward. Maybe the only way forward.

"A police constable – trainee role. It's for a start in April. The salary's not great, but it would be a step on the ladder, and it's more money than a student grant. Under the circumstances of this year, we might be able to negotiate for you to continue to live here until June. That would give you time to find some alternative accommodation for next year. Maybe a flat that you and Daniel could share?"

A look of confusion crosses her face. I glance at Dan and laugh at his expression of horror.

"I think Dan and I should live near each other, but if we were in the same flat, you'd have another murder to solve – mine."

"It wouldn't take you long to solve it." He sniffs, and gives a watery smile. "I love Becky like a sister, but I'm tidy and she's not. Shall we leave it at that? Seriously, though – I think it's a great idea, Becks, and you should take it up. Get yourself into the police force. Become independent. Tell your dad you're following your dreams. I wish I could say the same to mine."

NOT THE END

Fantastic Books
Great Authors

darkstroke is
an imprint of
Crooked Cat Books

- Gripping Thrillers
- Cosy Mysteries
- Romantic Chick-Lit
- Fascinating Historicals
- Exciting Fantasy
- Young Adult and Children's Adventures

Discover us online
www.darkstroke.com

Find us on instagram:
www.instagram.com/darkstrokebooks

Printed in Great Britain
by Amazon